Mourning Becomes the Hangman

Mourning Becomes the Hangman

MARK McSHANE

A CRIME CLUB BOOK
DOUBLEDAY
New York   London   Toronto   Sydney   Auckland

A Crime Club Book
PUBLISHED BY DOUBLEDAY
a division of Bantam Doubleday Dell Publishing Group, Inc.
666 Fifth Avenue, New York, New York 10103

DOUBLEDAY and the portrayal of a man
with a gun are trademarks of Doubleday,
a division of Bantam Doubleday Dell
Publishing Group, Inc.

Library of Congress Cataloging-in-Publication Data
McShane, Mark, 1930–
Mourning becomes the hangman / Mark McShane. — 1st ed.
p.   cm.
"A Crime Club book."
I. Title.
PR6062.O853M68   1991
823'.914—dc20   90-43775
                                                   CIP
ISBN 0-385-41760-8
Copyright © 1991 by Mark McShane
All Rights Reserved
Printed in the United States of America
March 1991
First Edition

Mourning Becomes the Hangman

ONE

Donald was impressed. It didn't matter now, following that first nudge of disappointment, the courtroom being far smaller than expected, he should have known there would be at least one aspect to jar. Everything else was perfect: the smell of polish and cough drops, the wood which had absorbed countless yesterdays of true drama, the wigs and gowns, the almost strokeable ambience of solemnity.

What impressed Donald most, however, was himself. Or rather, the fact that here he actually was, in the Old Bailey. He had known about it all his life. The name was as familiar to him as Big Ben or Tower Bridge or St. Paul's. But whereas elsewhere in the world you could find other famous clocks and bridges and cathedrals, who could tell you the name of another celebrated law court?

Rolling his shoulders slightly, petting hackles, Donald shuffled himself on the wooden settle with satisfaction. He did love a win.

His settle was behind the dock, with press and jury on the left, barristers gathered to the right, below the witness box. Straight ahead, lording it over all, pompous, rose the bench, mundane name for a site of power, its chairs so ponderous they moved on rails.

Some of the chairs were presently occupied. Three old men in exotic dress sat there trying to look wise, with those at the sides even having a star to follow—they, ornaments of tradition, leaving everything to the man in the middle, his lordship.

The half dozen other witnesses squeezed in with Donald, they sighed or mumbled. Donald became attentive. On seeing that the response had merely been to a change in speakers, theme still a drab point of law, he went back to being impressed.

Donald Morgan was a medium-built man of thirty-three with plentiful hair. He had a ruddy face of the cast that was called disarming when people wanted to avoid being kindly truthful and say insipid, or cruelly honest and say dumb. While no more a fair reflection of the accompanying mind than was any human face, save that of a moron, it did lean closer to truth than lie.

Donald's own idea of his appearance was every bit as flattering as a healthy-minded person's ought to be. Passingly, he felt he looked something like whichever cinema actor was his current favourite; permanently, he knew he had the stamp of an outdoorsman, the hearty non-smoking teetotaler who strides across fields with chin high and hard body in overalls.

Today Donald wore a suit in blue hopsack. It had been worn seldom in the five years since he had bought it, in 1945, to show his independence. The army-issue suit for demobilisation was a piece of rubbish, one of so obvious an origin that ex-soldiers often saluted each other in the street.

Donald still vaguely missed that, the saluting, pomp,

respect for rank. For a long time he had regretted not staying in the Forces, his Royal Engineers. He was sure that with his talent for inventing gadgets, his flair and those natural qualities of leadership, he would in time have become a captain.

Again murmurs offended, interrupting Donald's escape from the tedium that could lessen the impact of this grand occasion. His eyes reproachful, toastmaster locates cougher, he glanced up sourcewards at the public gallery, a space crammed tight with some forty people. They were watching the witness box.

Tensing, Donald looked down to see the woman leaving, her evidence given. He wondered if he would now have his turn. Suddenly he hoped not. It wasn't stage fright or fear of stammering or having to look at Henry Gosport, he insisted; it was just that he wanted to get thoroughly acclimatised here before being thrust into the limelight.

By shivering not unpleasantly at that, Donald was able to keep from admitting the truth, his reluctance to having the grand occasion over on the first day. He wanted it to last. The Gosport Case was on the front or second page of all the newspapers and he was an important part of it. Certainly, his name would be in the press. But that would be the end, once they had his evidence. He would be an outsider, no longer one of the privileged, and, with long queues waiting for the few public seats, he stood no chance of getting inside in any other capacity.

A voice called out a name.

One of the settle's people got up and Donald folded his arms tightly. Also he gave a small nod, as though to announce his agreement with the choice.

While taking over the box and being sworn in, the

witness looked everywhere except at the prisoner in the
dock. Noting this, Donald made a point for himself of
craning up boldly to see past the two guarding warders.
As before on sneaked glances, however, all he could see
was the rear head and shoulders of the man he thought of
as the murderer.

Relaxed, pleased, even owning a feeling of accomplishment, Donald served attention on the slow ask and tell
between witness and barrister. He allowed only brief re-
flective asides as to if they could only see him now, his
mother, his cousins, his wife, the neighbours.

Sir Percival Rangeway, counsel for the prosecution, was
tall and handsome, stately. He looked at ease in his wig,
not as if he thought he looked absurd. It pleased Donald
that they were, in a sense, on the same side. He made
disparaging comparisons with the fat defence lawyer and
tutted when at one stage he called out an objection.

The courteous way the tall barrister treated his witness
had Donald full of admiration. He was delighted to remind himself he had once considered a career at the bar,
which might have come to fruition if the war hadn't taken
him straight from grammar school and kept him for six
years.

Boy observes hero, Donald followed the prosecutor's
every utterance and gesture, nod and smile. He no longer
remembered how irked he had been to discover that, unlike what films had led him to believe, barristers in court
stood still instead of pacing dramatically, gown on the
billow. Donald was content.

When, presently, during a lull, he stopped being Sir
Percival Rangeway, it was to recall their meeting, their
only, at which the Queen's Counsel had taken him
through the questions he would be asked, by both prose-

cution and defence. It was no rehearsal, Donald defended, as though there had been that suggestion. Sir Percival had to know if his witness still held to the statement he had made weeks ago. In particular, he wanted to be sure he had seen Henry Gosport carrying a gun.

"Very definitely."

"It couldn't have been any other kind of object, Mr. Morgan?" the QC had asked, this followed by a list of possibles, each earning a negative. "So a gun it was."

"It was indeed, Sir Percival."

"But inside the house, in the dimness, you saw merely a shadow?"

"I'm afraid so."

The barrister had rustled his papers. "I'm sure we'll have enough to carry the day, Mr. Morgan. If ever a man deserved the noose, it's Gosport."

Donald closed out the recollection smartly, as though haste would cancel that last part. He felt awkward because he had failed to mention it to Alma, who would have said, "Why didn't you tell him you're opposed to capital punishment?" That would have spoiled it for him.

Lull over, Sir Percival Rangeway went back to examining the witness. Donald casually clasped his lapels.

Like the prince who doesn't discover the slavey to be plain until he gets her home, away from her ugly stepsisters, callers at Can Lane in Stepney were often fooled by contrasts. Some of its row houses still bearing the scars of German bombs, a few even roofless and dead-eyed, the untouched looked cozy and cute, old-fashioned, romantic.

This view died inside, through the door that opened directly from the pavement. A stench which only the poor fail to detect, that of poverty, was matched by rot, sleaze and the grime of indifference, as well as cooking odours beaten back inside by the backyard privy.

Number 10 reversed the pattern. Although shrapnel had pitted its face and time blistered its paint, the house inside was clean and cared about. Furthermore it had a bathroom, carpets, furniture chosen from good catalogues and one of the newest television sets with the big twelve-inch screen.

For those at the profession's bottom and top, crime generally pays its faithful well, and steadily, with no interruptions for prison. This is not because small-timers are beneath a policeman's contempt, being too easy to capture, but because that capture would win him no promotion, while with millionaire swindlers it isn't due so much to their being above his ambition or talent as to the fact that he rarely learns of the swindles.

Molly Harker dealt in stolen goods. They were clothing, domestic appliances, cutlery, watches, anything that could be moved with ease, anything for which there was a constant market. Seldom present in number 10, the goods changed hands via Molly-made introductions. She took a commission. The fee was as small as the risk yet enough to ensure financial comfort. If there was any police interest in Molly Harker it stemmed from her being the long-term mistress of a crook, Henry Gosport.

Molly was thinking about Henry as she walked across Stepney toward Can Lane. What else, she bullied, would she be thinking about today? If she had been able to get in the court she would be looking at him right now.

Though Molly pretended to be miffed, she had purposely left it too late to go to the Old Bailey. She didn't want to see her Henry in the dock, she had been through that one before often enough, God knew. She would tell him about it later.

Which, the later, would be another overseen visit, Molly greyly knew. Henry was sure to be sent down, a man with a record like his. Although they couldn't make the murder charge stick, he wouldn't get a day less than five years, not for robbery with violence. Discounting time off for GB, that meant three and a bit.

Sick of the repetition of thoughts she had lived with for weeks, Molly lengthened her stride and took comfort in another repetition: Should she get herself a nice little car?

She could take Johnny out into the country, she mused. Get some of that fresh air people were always on about, as if in Stepney the air was second-hand. If nothing else, a car would take the drudgery out of journeying to see Henry on those grim monthly visits.

Being so quickly back to that again, Molly had to laugh. It rang out hearty.

An ample blonde, Molly Harker had the bearing of someone who would just as soon say "piss off" as "hello." She leaned to flashy yet expensive clothes that farther west across London would have marked her as a whore, that in Stepney elected her to the level of dead smart. At thirty-five she was pretty enough to appear so even through the heavy cosmetics. Her bountiful jewellery she bought in Woolworth's, the same local store in which she had begun her shoplifting career at the age of eight, a calling she left behind at twenty on inheriting her mother's introduction service.

Molly entered Can Lane. Waving at one woman, making for another the V sign, she let herself into number 10. In the living kitchen at the back, uptaut pose gone, she gasped her way to the fulfillment of what she had been aching for since leaving the bus—a cigarette. A woman smoking in the street, as far as Molly was concerned, looked bloody common.

After a cup of tea she lit up again, so had a cigarette's support as, pacing, she allowed herself to worry about Henry, the man she loved, bane and joy of her life, father of her child.

In court would he get out of hand? Sneer at everyone? Take a poke at the warder? Tell the judge what he could do with his gavel? Or would he play the right dock rôle— mild, a bit bewildered, the simple man caught in a web of other folk's lies? It made such a difference. It could mean as much as a year less on the sentence, even more if you could manage a tear or two.

Molly had stopped pacing, was thinking of the years of lonely bed and board ahead, especially bed, when a noise sounded in the back yard. She tossed her cigarette end in the sink on passing to the door. Unlocked, it let in her son.

Johnny was seven years old, unlovely, scruffy. His smile showed twisted teeth and the cheek of a successful burglar. Over one eye zagged an angry graze, which made his mother give a cry. It was raucous enough to fit a razor slashing.

She ranted questions. "What's that? The other kids been at you? Who did it?" Pulling him inside she started to bathe the slight wound.

His smile on the wince, martyr gratified, Johnny explained about the slip during play. Molly, her heart settling from its run, told herself she might have known cause to be innocent. With his father on trial for murder, there was no child more popular in Stepney than Johnny Harker.

Graze clean and touched with iodine, mother took son on her knee to give the comfort she was in need of giving. She kissed him, stroked his hair, squeezed him hard to the accompaniment of groans, asked him who was the best boy in all the world, then.

By keeping patiently still Johnny showed what he was made of, as he saw it, for no tough kid going on eight could possibly enjoy being messed about by women.

Solace over, Molly sent her son off with a shilling to buy cakes while she set about making a meal of treat dimensions, which seemed only right.

Her thoughts went to the trial. They settled at length on the people who were giving evidence against Henry. As she sliced bread, knife sure in her hand, she dwelled on what she would like to do to those bastards and bitches, do with pleasure, then watch them in their gory throes of dying.

"Quick," Bran said, taking the woman's arm. "This way."

Startled, she gasped, "What's up?"

"Explain in a minute, Mrs. Wright. Come on. Look sharp."

She trotted beside him. "Well . . ."

He was helped, Bran knew, as he had been helped often before, by the fact that he looked like a policeman—at least, once that idea had been suggested. His build, raincoat and trilby were right, at thirty he was the usual middle-of-the-ladder age for a plain-clothes detective, his pleasing British looks seemed to be what people expected of someone dedicated to upholding law and order, the white knight fixation.

What pleased about Bran's looks was what would have

bored outside the Anglo-Saxon world. His skin was pale, his eyes were light blue and his blond hair had the curly animation of railway lines. But even your exotic woman would, on closer gaze, have found appeal in the combination of straight nose and insolent mouth.

Out of the building, Bran hurried Mrs. Wright along the street like a husband with a train for his wife to catch. His glances back showed no other reporters in pursuit. Perhaps, he thought, they saw no news value in the minor witness; and, he tacked on, perhaps they were right. The whole Gosport trial was turning out to be low on sensation.

Preferring to believe he had bested his colleagues, it always made them more bearable, Bran brought Mrs. Wright to a halt around the corner. "Here we are."

"What?"

"You get your breath back," he said without the previous severity, moving away. He went quickly to his car, got out the camera, strode back.

Bran loved that—striding. It never failed to make him feel as though big and relishy doings were at hand, the kind he had expected on asking to be moved from sport to the crime desk. As he should have known, and soon found out, crime was more exciting in print than in the street. But it still had the edge over cricket or football.

"Hold it. Thank you."

"I thought . . ." the fortyish woman began uncertainly when she had stopped blinking from the flash.

"Brandon Peel of the *Daily Standard*," Bran said, cordial. He held his face straight all but for crinkling the skin beside his eyes, politician with tired lips. "You, ma'am, are of great interest to our readers."

Uncertainty flourished. "The *Standard?*" Mrs. Wright

said. Her tone would have been more suitable to a question such as, "A pile of old rags?"

Far from being offended, Bran partly sympathised, and not only because he had started to become immune to the response through repetition. That the tabloid he worked for was short on everything except crudity and brashness, he accepted. Its lack of ethics he deplored, its deliberate insulting of the truth he despised. That its headline type was the largest among the national press he could have applauded if not for the fact that its apology/retraction type on page ten was microscopic. Daily he cringed at the newspaper's And-But style, with a story's second para starting with *And*, its third with *But*, which toenail journalism hurt him most when it was subbed into his own sound contributions.

The answer, as Bran knew so well, was to quit. He would have done so like a shot horse drops if he had thought he could get another job; a job, that is, as a reporter, the part he had always wanted to play, and currently played, and hoped to go on playing.

With no discomfort Bran knew he saw the newspaper world as glamorous, its leaders as titans, its subjects as romantic. That he didn't mind at all. What did bother him was a suspicion that this glitterview might be responsible for the loophole he clung to, his conviction that all he needed to enable him to escape from the *Ands* and *Buts* of tabloidism—be wanted by quality editors—was the large scoop of daydreams.

Bran hoped his loophole had more solidity than a mirage. He believed it had. Clowns did play Hamlet and those trumpet-backed searchlight-washed scoops did happen, he knew, so he was wise in continuing to try all angles and outwit the opposition, even if it didn't make him the most popular man in Fleet Street, though it sometimes did make him the silliest.

"No, I wasn't nervous," the woman said.

"Were the questions what you expected?"

"Yes. I have to be running along now."

Ignoring that: "You're obviously a very brave woman, Mrs. Wright. Your husband must be proud of you."

"I'm a widow."

Bran performed that slow nodding with head one degree aslant, the mime which told, *Suddenly I find you more interesting.* The woman went pink on her neck. His phoniness Bran excused as readily as he had his change of name from Jack to Brandon, it being all part of the trade, as well as flattering to the recipient.

"Anyway," he said, "now you've given your evidence, you're free to make any statement you want."

Neck in hand: "Yes, I know."

"So what d'you think about Gosport, Mrs. Wright? Is he guilty of murder?"

"Oh yes. No doubt of it. Not in my mind anyway."

"That's what most people say."

"You know how it all came about, of course," the woman said, revealing her neck.

"Yes I do. Every detail."

But Mrs. Wright, obviously, wanted to talk to the interested party, embellish that same interest with what lately must have made her the envy of her friends. Although Bran sighed, hidingly down his nose, he acknowledged he had no one to blame but himself.

Mr. Arnold Cross took his restaurant's weekly takings home in a briefcase every Friday evening, banking Saturdays. On the second Friday in September, ignoring that the date was the thirteenth, he went by taxicab as usual to his detached house in Putney, arriving at the gate safely. The taxi had gone and Cross was letting himself into the house, his wife being out, when two men appeared on the short driveway. At a rush they followed Arnold Cross into his home. There was the sound of shouts and scuffling. Silence came after a shot was fired. Entering as the silence went on, neighbours and passers-by found Cross lying dead, a gun on the floor along with a bloody ornamental sword belonging to the householder, the briefcase of money gone and the back door open, no one living present.

An hour later a known criminal, Charles Grew, who had been released from prison three days before after serving a sentence for armed robbery, staggered into Emergency at Hammersmith Hospital with a deep gash in his chest. He died before they could get him on the operating table.

Next day, acting on selections from Records at Scotland Yard by witnesses at the Cross house, police identified Charles Grew as one of the robbers and in raids around London picked up seven men, whom they put in separate identity parades. All witnesses pointed out the same suspect, Henry Gosport.

Under questioning Gosport at first denied involvement in the affair. Following a talk with his solicitor, however, he admitted to having been on the scene of the crime, though in an innocent capacity. He said he had been drinking with Grew, who had startled him by saying he was going to commit a robbery. Gosport did his best to dissuade him. He continued to try as Grew, medium drunk, left the pub, and, a little drunk himself, even tried to stop him physically, following right to the house and inside.

"What a fairy story," the woman said.

"But not impossible."

"Well, that's true, that's true."

"There was only the one gun found."

"He took the other with him, you can bet. He had plenty of time to get rid of it, didn't he?"

"I suppose," Bran said.

"The river. That's where your gangsters throw their guns. And Henry Gosport's a true-blue gangster all right."

"I wonder."

"Why, he even admitted that the only reason he tried to stop Grew was because he'd just come out of prison and should have a bit of freedom before he got into more trouble, otherwise he wouldn't have bothered."

"Actually, that attitude, that kind of honesty, works in Gosport's favour."

"It's all a pack of lies," Mrs. Wright said. She was getting uncertain again.

Entertaining defeat in his attempt to goad the outrageous, newsy, Bran shifted his heavy camera from one arm to the other and said, "A final question, ma'am. If Arnold Cross had lived, do you think he ought to have been charged with murder?"

"Oh, I don't know about that. Myself, I'm not one to make judgements. Now I really do have to be running along. Shall I give you my address?"

At twenty-nine years of age Alma Morgan had the assurance of the manageress she would surely have become had she stayed in business, not married Donald. Also she owned the under-manner of one who knew she had made the right move. It showed even without her excesses of humming around the house, taking good care of her fingernails and not complaining when it never stopped raining. Alma had taken to country life in a way that any sane countrywoman would have found offensive.

Slim, she was wiry and vigorous in pursuit of a chore's conquest, fragile in the creation of a tender moment, though should that moment extend to the erotic she could bring out her vigour to reach the summit.

Alma had short fair hair, eyes of furious blue, curved eyebrows which she plucked in secret. Her face was rendered pretty by a combination of immature features, a good smile and the plaintive aspect that, as an orphan, she early on had felt obliged to cultivate because it seemed expected.

Alma was looking out of the living room window at a view of apple trees. Morgan Orchards surrounded the house to an extent of twenty acres, all getting close to being paid for, thanks to hard slogging and scientific methods. Alma was almost as proud of that as she was of near-success coming without having given in and asked for a loan from Donald's mother, who had shaken her head at the venture with a musical, "You'll see what you'll do."

The grandfather clock chimed. Turning, Alma amused herself by strolling around the room instead of making a straight line. There were large old pieces of furniture to circle, all bought at auction, the new post-war stuff being trash; in any case, the doddery house would have been made to look shabby by new innards, whereas herewith it passed for quaint.

In front of a sideboard mirror Alma took up a brush and treated her hair to firm strokes. She avoided her eyes, as do people who have nothing to hide, fearful of being made to feel dull by the lack of intrigue. Next she put on a touch of pink lipstick.

Once she had left the mirror Alma laughed at herself, along with a handclap. It was of course ridiculous to tart yourself up to speak to someone on the telephone, which was why she laughed, glad of her silliness. Frequently Alma considered herself to be just a little too much on the sensible side.

It was necessary, she pampered. Someone here had to keep two feet on the turf. Donald, apart from the orchard, did tend to be floating on cloud three, especially with his wild schemes and elaborate plans.

Circling the room, Alma came to her husband's defence, which she would not have done if he had been at home, even unseen up in his den. Unrecognised decency produced the reminder, in equal truth, that Donald was reliable. Good man to have around in a crisis. And if most of his schemes withered on the vine—what of that? They were harmless enough and no one got hurt. There was a plus in his enthusiasms being attractive and infectious. Currently, there was fun in knowing how much he was enjoying these few days in London.

Glancing at the grandfather clock, Alma held up both hands with their fingers crossed to help in hoping her husband would remember to reverse the charges, otherwise their talk was sure to be cut off, coins running out.

While awaiting the call-signal Alma continued circling the large room and pictured different versions of Donald leaving the Old Bailey, walking to his hotel, asking to use the telephone. In one version he was stopped on the street by a prostitute. With a kind shake of his head he went on.

Recognising this sub-plot for what it was, a reaffirmation of the halo she had given her husband, in serious jest, Alma smiled broadly. In addition she was gladdened by having true appreciation of herself.

The telephone rang.

Stopping, Alma looked over at the instrument in an act of light surprise, which idiocy was to milk that appreciation. She snapped normal and went across to answer.

Would Mrs. Donald Morgan accept a call . . .

She would.

Donald said, "Hello, darling."

"Hello, darling," Alma said, lifting her shoulders and cuddling the receiver affectionately.

More standard exchanges over, Donald began on reporting his day in court. No, he hadn't been called yet. Tomorrow for sure. But things were going well.

Although aware of being invisible to her husband, Alma kept her smile on the inside of her mouth at his proprietory way of talking, as if he were the prosecution's owner; also at the tone and language he adopted for certain retailings, now for an angle on the briefcase.

"It has been established, at least to the satisfaction of any intelligent person, that Henry Gosport was observed following the event with a briefcase in his possession. He was alone and running."

"He claimed he had been helping Charles Grew, no? That Grew had the briefcase and let it fall."

"And that he, the accused, disregarded it. An obvious lie. The man is a member of the underworld. He would hardly be party to the abandonment of several thousand pounds."

Alma said, "They did find it later."

"Empty, darling. Accused said he imagines someone must have come across it and appropriated the funds."

"If I recall, there were no fingerprints on the case."

"Exactly," Donald said, heavy as relief. "A tempted passer-by, being non-criminal, would undoubtedly have left prints. Accused wore gloves, obviously."

Though she didn't agree that a passer-by wouldn't have had enough sense to wipe the briefcase, Alma let it lie. She said, "Anyway, darling, that doesn't have a lot of bearing on the main, capital issue."

"It is after the fact, true. On that other side, I personally believe that we'll get a manslaughter verdict from the jury. There'll be no work for the hangman."

"I was thinking about that this afternoon. I came up with a wonderful scheme. Remind me to tell you tomorrow night. No, I'll tell you now."

"Anti–capital punishment?" Donald asked, Alma not missing the tinge of sulkiness, limelight lost. Sympathising, she made it brief in explaining that what somebody could do was pretend to murder his wife, who would go into hiding after they had planted clues pointing to him. He would be arrested, tried, found guilty and sentenced to death.

"Then, when the last appeal had failed, out wifey would pop." At phrasing so flippantly what she had thought on with cautious care, Alma felt warm on her chest.

Donald said it was a neat idea. "And after that we had the ballistics man."

"That must've been fascinating."

"But I'd better not rattle on. We're going to have a monster phone bill. There is one other thing though. The newspapers in the morning. Well anyway, the *Standard*."

"Yes, darling?"

At the way her husband's voice developed a leisure, even an exhaustion, to tell about the reporter who had taken his picture, which would be in the morning edition, Alma allowed her smile to come out to play. Anyone would think he was sick to death of having his photograph in the national press, she mused. Donald was lovely.

After closing the front door Molly took three paces to the window. Its curtains not quite meeting, she peered through the crack into the lighted parlour, where Johnny sat watching television. She wriggled her chin close to her neck in the satisfaction of knowing Johnny was bathed and combed, clean of teeth and wearing a dressing gown which had come from the most exclusive clothing store in Scotland, according to the shoplifter.

With less satisfaction, yet not lacking an undertow of gleeful pride in the inherited cunning, Molly knew her son was aware of being watched; aware of the fact that "slipping up to the Coach for a quick drink" meant a prolonged stay; aware of the chocolate biscuits hidden in the kitchen. He would gorge and watch too much telly and play about, and, hours past the bed-time he had sworn with aching sincerity to honour, would dart upstairs on hearing his mother's approach.

Feeling like Saturday night, Molly walked on. Normally she would not be going out midweek. But a public appearance was more or less expected during these harrowing days. People who felt shy about calling at the house under ongoing circumstances, who felt that a certain speechifying formality would have to be observed, could in a pub express themselves via nods and winks, pats and nudges, the quiet dicky-bird in passing and the drink sent across in pseudo-anonymity, barmaid whispering, "It's on Jim but he said not to say."

As Molly was turning out of Can Lane a car came to a rumbled halt at her side. The driver, sole occupant, looked up at her with a bright, "Miss Harker, isn't it?" He kept pace and went on talking when she held to her walk without a pause. She could smell a reporter almost as surely as she could a policeman.

Not until the man, fat and bronchial, was becoming less polite in his opportuning did Molly stop. She leaned down. Softly she told him that if he wanted to have his spinal column damaged it could be arranged, no charge. Straightening, she walked on. The car stayed where it was.

In the Coach and Horses, fuggy as a fiction dive, other customers called out greetings to Molly as she crossed to the bar. There she ordered a gin and didn't scramble into her bag for cigarettes until it was served. Inhaling smoke, glass in hand, she heavied her eyelids in thanks for a kind of fulfillment.

An hour later, Molly broke off her talk with a friend at yet another tap on the shoulder. The smile she turned with, it went cynical, lover finds fault, when she saw the tapper was not only a stranger but possibly a reporter.

"Brandon Peel of the *Daily Standard,*" he said, polite. "Good evening, Miss Harker."

Dead: "What you want?"

"I wondered if we could have a chat. I'm covering the Gosport trial. Maybe there's something you'd like to get off your chest. You know?"

"There's millions of things, sonny, but I don't like reading about myself in newspapers."

"Oh? Why's that?"

"Somehow, people's words get twisted wrong way round by you lot."

While the man was doing the expected, selling himself

as purer than midnight snow, his attitude bearing the element of grovel that she so enjoyed, Molly was taking in his attractiveness. Inside her, she had a familiar clench of sexuality.

It had been a long time. It was going to be even longer. But maybe this time she would have a go on the q.t. She could hook up with some nice strong type from another manor. They could have good old dirty weekends in Southend.

Molly had been through this before. It never came to carnal grips because, first, she was the faithful kind, and second, she knew Henry would finish with her for good if he found out, after he had beaten her unconscious. Beating she could take, no novelty that; Henry she wouldn't be able to bear losing. She would kill to keep the truth from him. But then, there wasn't going to be any truth to keep back.

Grunting at herself, Molly gave her attention fully to the reporter, who was praising his paper as the most honourable in the field. Airy, she cut in, "Yes, yes, you can have your chat. I'll be with you in a minute."

"Thank you," he said. "I'll wait over here."

"I might be half an hour."

"That's fine, Miss Harker."

As he moved away, heading for a table, Molly accepted that she was doing this only because she fancied the stranger. She had a craving for attention from an attractive male. She could sit so this one would have a good view up her legs. A cheap thrill was better than no thrill at all.

Within ten minutes Molly was sharing a table with the newspaper man, her lower body unseeable, which position she had watched herself assume with a mixture of sniffed approval and gaunt resignation.

The reporter had gone straight to the night of the Cross robbery. "Did you have an inkling, Miss Harker, of what was going to happen?"

"How could I?"

"Well, you and Henry Gosport are—um—"

"He's my common-law husband," Molly said. "What I meant was, how could I have an inkling when Henry had no inkling himself. He got mixed up in this by accident, remember."

"Ah, well, yes."

She hadn't known he had gone on a job, he hadn't said, as normal, aware that she would fuss and worry. It was on recalling his curious stiffness on leaving that she had rushed to the hiding place to count guns. There was one missing.

"Why did Henry Gosport go out the back way at the robbery scene, Miss Harker?"

"He had to follow his mate to help him, dint he, after he'd been mortally wounded by that Arnold Cross, what poor Charlie'd had to shoot in self-defence."

Since they were talking on serious matters, Molly mused, the quiet way he smiled at her could only mean the reporter was letting her know he fancied her. That was better than a kick in the shin any old day.

The reporter asked, "But didn't Charles Grew arrive at the hospital alone?"

"Henry saw him to the door and then took off," Molly said, glaring because as far as she knew it was true. "It was all nothing to do with him, after all." She stopped glaring.

"I wonder what became of the money."

She had been pacing the kitchen in a stew of worry

when Henry's young brother came with the word he had just got on the blower from Henry. There was a gun and a briefcase. They had been dropped in the front garden of 66 Archer Street, Putney. Go there at once. Wear gloves. Collect gun and money but leave case.

Molly said, "Some thieving sod nicked it, no doubt."

"No doubt."

"But I will tell you one thing, and you can quote me."

The reporter leaned forward. "Yes?"

"My Henry will never try to do a mate a favour again."

Reversing: "I see."

After squashing out a cigarette in the ashtray Molly lifted her arms in a stretch. With the jacket shifting aside, her silky blouse was thrust into view by her breasts, at which the reporter looked while Molly looked at the reporter, until he lifted his eyes to hers, when, before glancing aside, she showed him the tip of her tongue.

As Molly lowered her arms, clenching inside, the man said, "Nice tits." She pretended not to hear. That was as far as it could go, she was pleased and furious to acknowledge, again playing deaf to the suggestion that they finish their chat somewhere else, such as in his car.

Molly got up. She said a cool good-night and moved away with hips that seemed to be performing provocation of their own accord. Back at the bar she lit a fresh cigarette and through mirrors watched drably as the reporter left.

Oh, for the exciting, romantic life of a gangster's girl friend, she thought, with champagne and night clubs and all the frills. What a load of balls.

However, Molly gradually cheered up, for the only gathering whose central figure can stay uncharmed by the attention is a wake. She told people what a drag it was always being pestered by the press, she enjoyed the piano playing and sing-song, she accepted winks, smiles, nudges, quiet words in passing and the drinks that came courtesy of anonymous Bills or Janes or Nellies.

"You said in your statement, Mr. Morgan, that you saw Grew and Gosport running up the driveway."

"That's right."

"Sorry to bore you with the repetition of all this, by the way," Chief Inspector Jones said. "I won't take long."

Honestly: "I don't mind at all."

"Cheers. Nice sherry."

"Cheers. Thank you."

"Now, Mr. Morgan. It was dusk but the street lamps were on, so you could see with fair clarity."

"Well, only just," Donald said. "And it was from the back, of course. They were running away from where I was standing, on the pavement."

"You couldn't see, then, what they were carrying."

"Not really. Not quite."

Chief Inspector Jones, white haired, brown spotted, took several anxious pulls on his meerschaum, stopping when he had won a seep of smoke. Anxiety gone, he said:

"Just as well, Mr. Morgan. If we could use your evidence it would mean you having to come to London. You'd have to appear in the famous Old Bailey."

Donald said, "Oh?"

"Also some people don't like being a household word up and down the country, what with radio and press and God knows what all. They prefer privacy."

"I know what you mean."

"Your posh hotel would, naturally, be paid for, as well

as all other expenses, but it would still be taking you away from your apple trees. Lovely place, this."

"Thank you."

Another seep of smoke won, Chief Inspector Jones said, "Anyway, let's have this finished with. I believe some of the other witnesses said the killers turned aside as they ran. More than once. As they would, naturally enough, to check on the safety or otherwise at the rear. I suppose you do recall that, Mr. Morgan, the killers turning aside."

"Well yes, I seem to. Yes, I do."

"And with them turning to the right, as right-handed people do, turning, in fact, toward the light, you must have seen what they were holding, just as the other witnesses did. Guns, they stated. Right, Mr. Morgan?"

"Well, yes. Right."

"You saw plenty of guns in the army, I dare say."

"Oh, plenty."

"So you couldn't be mistaken, could you? Course not. I do believe I'll have another spot of your excellent sherry, Mr. Morgan."

Donald had been cued to replay the scene by dwelling again on his photograph. It had appeared in this morning's edition of the *Daily Standard*, on page four. Two inches square, showing him striding away from the Old Bailey, face serious, it was captioned, "Mr. Ronald Morgan, one of the witnesses for the prosecution in the Gosport Case."

That they had got his name wrong Donald didn't mind in the least, he had mused often since coming back from buying the newspaper, sometimes lifting his shoulders. Not in the least. Not at all. No.

Another such musing Donald ended now by looking around. He reminded himself how much he was enjoying his stay here. The small hotel had what your four- or five-star places lacked—friendly staff, no starch, comfort.

Donald finished his coffee. Nodding on the repeat information that he could correct the misprint with Indian ink before putting the clipping into his scrapbook, he slid the folded newspaper into his pocket. That he had no idea whether the photograph was on the outside or not was a dessert for his breakfast.

Donald got up from the table. With semi-bows for those guests who were not new today, who knew exactly where he was going, a less pronounced bow toward the woman who was finished, done, her evidence given, he walked out of the dining room.

Outdoors, Donald cooled from the way he had reacted with hot prickles to the woman's smile. In any event, he distantly acknowledged, he could have been wrong. Her smile might simply have been friendly, not what he had thought, a snide reference to the caption's inaccuracy. That is, misprint. It could also have been rue that he made no mention of her own photograph, on the same page.

Donald walked at an exaggeration of his customary bold snap, the stand-back-there of authority. It occurred to him that if he were to drop dead at this very moment—well, he wouldn't mind all that much.

He was almost sorry to arrive.

Through dawdling out front, where a small crowd had gathered, Donald was late inside. No sooner had he sat than he had to get to his feet again for the entry of his lordship. The court was in session.

Two interesting hours later a voice called out, "Donald Frederick Morgan."

Instantly, Donald was shattered. He saw once more that

green child-crammed room in the free dental clinic and heard the man in charge bellow the next victim's name.

At equal speed, Donald recovered, and to so complete an extent that he had a blitheness as he entered the witness box. The oath he took with ringing tones.

Next he was looking down at Sir Percival Rangeway, who was saying, "Let me read out your statement, Mr. Morgan."

While the rich voice filled in background leading to his business trip to Putney that evening, Donald, after looking most other places, suddenly turned his eyes on the man who was standing in the box opposite.

Henry Gosport had the sturdy frame of an unskilled labourer. His face, crudely handsome, was that of a fading gigolo. He wore the broad-shouldered suit favoured by costermongers and crooks. His manner could have belonged to a priest who, having stumbled into a den of vice, wonders not so much how he can get quickly out as what people see in it. He was forgiving. In the set of his head lay a suggestion that he could weep for the folly of it all.

Gosport's gaze met Donald's and held it steadily, mild as young milk. Donald felt his apprehension start to shrink. Before he could finish thinking he didn't know what he had been worried about, he was telling himself it was a good job he wasn't the type to worry. Henry Gosport, plainly, had no personal feelings about the witnesses.

Donald looked away. He was happy to return his attention to the barrister to whom, he had started to believe, he bore a slight resemblance.

"Is that correct, Mr. Morgan?"

"Yes, it is."

"Fine," Sir Percival Rangeway said, uncle to clever nephew. "By which time you had arrived at the gate of Mr. Arnold Cross's residence. You stopped there on hearing the sound of running. Is that correct?"

"Yes, it is."

It went on. Kindly, caressingly, with a forward lean that was almost a salaam in answer to every affirmative, the Queen's Counsel brought his witness along. In referring to Donald's military experience he called him a war hero no more than four times, voice lowered. He gestured like a blessing. When once defence counsel objected, he said a humble, "Quite so. I withdraw the question." His every look at the ten men and two women showed how grateful he was for their intelligence.

"You had taken several steps along the drive, Mr. Morgan, were therefore closer to the open door. Could you see through it with fair clarity?"

Only too glad to be accommodating, Donald said an emphatic, "Yes I could."

"The pair of intruders, after the skirmish of a fast arrival inside, turned to the right or the left?"

"Right. That's where Mr. Cross had gone."

"Precisely," Sir Percival said. "I want you to think carefully about your answer to my next question, Mr. Morgan. Will you do that?"

"I will, yes."

"Were the intruders in the same order as before, outside, Charles Grew in the lead?"

From a slant of eyebrow and a quirk of mouth it was clear that the question struck its asker as mildly amusing; as not necessary; as one to which only a fool or a blackguard would answer with anything but a firm negative.

Donald said, "He was not, no."

"In fact, Henry Gosport was first, gun in hand?"

"That is correct."

Sir Percival Rangeway did his salaam. "Thank you, Mr. Morgan. That will be all."

If there is one point on which everyone is exactly the same, it is that he thinks himself different. Bran Peel was no exception. Growing up bland in a lower middle-class suburb, where, though morals might be as tainted as the cut-price groceries everyone bought, front curtains were always clean, he knew there was a more florid world somewhere else and that he could be a part of it. He was, after all, unique.

This Bran had proved to himself in various ways. He embraced atheism at choir practice, he had a fondness for studying, he disliked smoking and motor-cycles, he declined to go to university after winning a scholarship, his copy for the advertising agency was original, he had no guilt about having spent the war years in munitions work as a conscientious objector, his skill at avoiding marriage never flagged.

Therefore Bran did, in a sense, own proof of his uniqueness. A brief no more specious than anyone else's, it had allowed him to accept without embarrassment that he was headed for great things in his chosen field. It was a case not so much of this being predestined, he felt, as deserved. He was different.

Meanwhile, Bran went on cleaving to the conviction that a scoop was the way to a journalistic top where all was so florid you had to take time off twice a year to go to a health farm; went on being satisfied with his 1937 Austin 12; went on denying that he didn't mind coming home to the empty flat in Pimlico.

He closed the door with a slam. Pulling off his hat he sailed it above the untidiness to a neat landing on a table of clothes like a bring-and-buy. When he turned to the corner kitchenette—stove and sink—he was thinking about Molly Harker, as he had on and off throughout the day.

You couldn't blame him, Bran had defended at one stage. The woman herself apart, you had to do something with your mind to stay awake during what some of the press boys were calling ironically the sleeper of the year.

That his carnal interest in Gosport's mistress had been returned by her Bran considered as he waited for the stew to get warm. He admitted he relished the flattery of that and would enjoy seeing her again, even if nothing happened in respect of sex, which was unlikely, she being so obviously on, hot, ready. For the right man, of course. But the flattery would be nice in itself.

The question of whether or not to make contact Bran left on getting his dinner organised. He sat with a tray on his knees in front of the gas fire, which he lit for the company. He thought about work.

The Central Criminal Court, better known as the Old Bailey, was the scene today of a pleasant break in tedium. No, that would never do, Bran allowed. Dear Pulp Reader had to be given a hotted-up version, otherwise he could start buying a different tabloid. *The vivid trial of Henry Gosport took on extra steam during cross-examination?*

It had been lively, right enough, Bran thought. Defence counsel had made apple crumble out of the orchard keeper and mush of his evidence.

So you can see in the dark, eh, Mr. Morgan? Even over a long distance? I should imagine that was what made you a hero during the war. How many medals did you get?

What, not a single one? Shame! Disgrace! Something must be done! What? Oh, I see, you were not a hero. So *that* was why you didn't rush to the victim's aid when you could see with such wonderful clarity that he was being attacked. Perhaps it wasn't all that clear to you, eh, Mr. Morgan?

Nice job of testimony destruction, Bran conceded, even though Donald Morgan himself had stood up to it well, going all colours without once getting angry or flustered. But it was another blow for the prosecution's case, and now the defence was going to get to work.

Would that mean more of that lively action?—Bran wondered without enthusiasm. He shrugged. The question he gave up to return to that other: the pursuit of Molly Harker.

Bran knew already, however, that he would make no effort to seek Gosport's girl friend out. He was teasing himself. Although he accepted that a man chose a woman for the mystery, for what might happen to be between her ears, not because of what he knew for a fact lay between her legs, he saw that in this case the challenge of a sharp mind would soon weaken: he was bound to discover limitations to the sharpness: girl friends of small-time crooks could hardly have far horizons. Once you lost respect for a mind, the body it controlled quickly became irrelevant.

Bran grunted. He put his unfinished dinner aside, slumped in the chair, stared at the fire. He had grown as bored with thoughts of Molly Harker as he was with her boy friend's trial, with warmed-over stew, and with trying to make useable significance out of the Old Bailey's dome-crowning statue of Justice being the only one in the world without a blindfold.

Unique, Bran thought, like me. He grinned with out-thrust jaw by way of denying that his eyes were blinking slowly as he sympathised with himself.

After lighting a slim, cheap cigar, Bran cast about inside for a suitable reverie to follow while his eyes fed on the gas flames. Our man in Moscow? Interview with the deposed king? Hold the front page?

Although Bran smiled at this, it didn't stop him, choice made, from proceeding with a cozy daydream.

Alma headed away from the orphanage. She drove at a steady, calm speed, the way people do when they want to show themselves how steady and calm they are, have become. They ignore that in their true state of being so they drive in a totally different manner.

Rashly was how Alma had driven at her most cautious moments three hours ago, heading in the opposite direction. She had abused the near-new Bradford van as though there were no more payments to be made. Her seethe had been so acute, she now kept tapping herself on the brow.

Alma's visits to the orphanage, which she never saw as the equivalent of going home to mother, were not confined to post-fight times. Since, being a secret romantic, she believed anniversaries had meaning, she sometimes went on her birthday. Not that anyone was there nowadays dating from her own childhood residence. But it was good to see house and grounds looking spruce, children and staff looking whole. She was always made welcome, furthermore, especially if she exaggerated her position in the world so they could tell each other on both age levels how well she had got on, this foundling, it just went to show. There was always someone to talk to.

This time Alma had sat in the garden with a twixt-lessons teacher who was only too happy to listen in trade for an ear: her own grievances with the gym instructor.

In talking about the latest strife with Donald ("Sometimes I could kill him") Alma had at length come to view the matter from her husband's angle so thoroughly that she had felt no annoyance at having to relinquish her sense of outrage.

She had been insensitive. She had been blind as a bat. She had failed to see how Don was feeling. She hadn't understood that, after being involved in high drama in no less a place than exciting London, he was still getting used to life back in the country.

Having taken what had seemed to be surliness as a personal affront, cause obscure, Alma had tried to force the matter out with pressure, like squeezing a boil, using the most common motive of their rare arguments, her husband's current inspiration or gadgetry infatuation.

"Darling," she had said, "there's no such thing as a machine for pruning trees. You're wasting your time."

"I should never've told you."

"You mean you think I'm too dense to understand?"

"You said that, not me."

It got worse.

Now Alma tapped her brow at how she had slammed out of the house, hurling behind her a final shout that it wouldn't be so pathetic if he ever actually got around to finishing one of his stupid schemes.

The two-hour drive to Cranwell village took seven years, the ten-minute run from there out to Morgan Orchards used up a fortnight. Alma ran in the house slowly.

There being no sight or sound of her husband downstairs, she checked bedrooms at a speedy dawdle and then his den/sanctuary, the attic. No answer to her knock, she plodded hurriedly down the two flights and outside, where she heard whistling. She felt her body relax.

Men whistled to keep their spirits up not out of defiance, Alma reminded herself more than once as she aimed for the Gilbert and Sullivan, strolling quickly.

"Donald?" she called, hat thrown in the door.

"Over here."

She came in sight of her husband. He was spraying the trunks of saplings. At Alma's approach he waved, calling, "Jury's out."

"Good," Alma said like a pat. Her face she kept downturned until she stood beside him. At the same time they both blurted, "Sorry about . . ."

What followed was as silly, sweet, moist and wonderful as innocence, as the purity to which its participants were returned. Even the self-reviling each indulged had a charm due to its enjoyment being so manifest.

If they had been indoors, Alma knew, they would have been on their way to bed by now. Herself, she would have been delighted to strip off right here and get on with it, but Donald tended to primness in matters of sex and she would no more have had him know of her greater earthiness than she would confess to plucking her eyebrows. She made do with stroking across the underside of his shoulder-blades.

Alma helping to spray, talk aiding that help, the work was soon done. They fettled the equipment and walked to the house holding hands, arms swinging.

Being nice, Alma said, "The jury's out, eh?"

"At three o'clock, the wireless said."

"We'll have it on again later, the news."

In his courtroom voice Donald said, "There'll be no guilty verdict. Not of murder."

"You ought to know, darling."

"Oh well."

They split to pass a tree, joined again. Alma said, "So this time there'll be no hanging."

"Not even life."

"I do wish someone would try my fabulous plot. I told you about it on the phone, remember?"

"I do, yes," Donald said warmly, the nice returned. "It's very neat. Your man gets himself arrested for killing his wife, then she turns up alive. Very neat indeed."

"Thank you." She squeezed his hand. It had nothing to do with the compliment.

"Only one thing to worry about."

"Tell me."

"No corpus delicti, darling."

"Don't need one," Alma said promptly. She reminded him of minor music hall entertainer Gay Gibson, who had disappeared from an ocean liner bound for South Africa. "They found the steward guilty of putting her through the porthole after killing her. He was hanged."

"So he was, by crikey," Donald said. Following a burst of whistling he went on, "Also, when your wife comes out of hiding in time to stop the execution, she's going to be in trouble."

"Whatever for?"

"She must've committed some kind of offence, fooling the law like that."

"She could claim she'd lost her memory. A cup of tea before I start to cook?"

"Righto."

They went in the house. Rejoining her husband in the

living room after putting the kettle on, Alma said, "Of course, I realise you're not as strong about it as I am, darling, the anti–capital punishment thing."

"Well, there's degrees, darling. No? Punishment fitting the crime and all that."

"I agree that hanging's too good for some killers."

Donald said, "Oh?"

Giving him his own major argument, a cliché, Alma said, "What about the man, a sane man, who rapes and murders a little girl? Her family would live with the pain of that memory every day of their lives. Not the killer. He'd escape through a noose into oblivion. That's not fair."

"Yes yes," Donald said, scratching his ribs, bodytalk more than drone stating that he was getting bored.

Alma asked, "Know where I went today, darling?"

When the subject appeared again, at supper, it came by radio. On hearing toward the end of the news broadcast, "At the Old Bailey this afternoon . . ." Alma and Donald looked at each other, slanted their heads toward the radio set, raised taut forefingers. They settled normal again after hearing of Henry Gosport being sentenced to two years hard labour as an accessory before the fact.

Flatly Donald said, "That's that." His manner was the one he used when condemning a scheme for having let him down.

"Yes," Alma said.

TWO

Fourteen months and two weeks after being sentenced, Henry Gosport was released from prison, term served.

Molly Harker didn't go to meet him at the gate. She never had done, after any of his previous convictions. The type of person Molly knew and accepted herself to be no more went to a prison on release morning than she asked her man what he had thought of the food.

Molly had several reasons for not waiting at the gate. The presence there of onlookers made reunion awkward; having a fair amount of true drama in her life with its caution and secrets, furtive meetings and danger, she felt no need to encourage the melodramatic; professional criminals being exquisite snobs, with a thousand levels to consider between mugger and confidence trickster, they couldn't countenance a rendezvous that would stamp them as amateurs.

In addition, with Molly herself, prosaically, she had to get Johnny off to school.

That done, she bathed and put on the clothes she had bought especially, some even from shops. She was open-handed with scent and jewellery and cosmetics. Her thrum of excitement was increased by a tinge of the illicit, for in order to have Johnny away in school she had lied about the release date of his father, whom he would find as a surprise treat at noon, better than going through the ache of waiting, waiting.

Ready, Molly lit a cigarette. She sat elegantly by the fire and glared around the room as though daring it to untidy itself. In time she cut off yet another glance at the mantelpiece clock, knowing you could go stark raving that way. Comfortably letting her elegance go, actress exits left, she told herself what a year it had been, by Christ.

What Molly settled on, after nods at the punch-up with the woman next door, Johnny's broken finger, her determined hunts for a suitable sex partner, who, once found, was given the slip before things got scorchy, and various golden middleman deals, was her visit to Morgan Orchards.

Wife had been cool. "Top floor. He's busy inventing. Go up." Husband had been cooler. He went on treading a foot-pump, blowing air into the tubes that served as posts on a slowly rising camper's tent while she explained about the Appeal.

He asked, "And?"

"I thought you might like to help, Mr. Morgan."

"I don't understand you."

"Look," she said. "If you was to go back on your evidence, admit you'd been a bit wrong like about a couple of things, it'd be real useful."

Pumping: "But I wasn't wrong. Why should I lie?"

Getting cool herself: "You lied before, in court, as you know very well."

"Are you accusing me of committing perjury?"

"Either that or you was badly mistaken. What counts is, it wasn't true what you said."

"I think it's time you were on your way."

Molly was seeing Donald Morgan take her curtly downstairs, her elbow gripped like a neck's scruff, when she heard brakes squeal out in the street.

Dog leaps for throat, Molly shot up from the chair. She stood taut for a wonderful moment of sweet cruelty before going out to the passage and along to the front door. She drew it open. Henry was paying off the taxi.

Molly stayed inside on the threshold, eyes down, giving nothing away in case, early though it might be, there were other eyes in the street. Emotion's not for sharing.

Henry came in. He edged past her with a whiff of government mothballs. When she joined him in the back room he was looking down into the fire, standing loose, allowing himself to end the act of a hard man coming back home from prison, cave in a little, even weep.

That he didn't do. Nor did Molly. Molly didn't cry until noon, following a meal and a mutual sex attack on the hearthrug, when Johnny came boistering in and flung to a stop like hitting a wall. Seeing her son's face, feeling the pain of the lump growing in his throat, Molly panted into tears and ran from the room.

In the afternoon they all went to the pictures.

Life was normal again at 10 Can Lane, at least for the woman of the house. For the males it took longer to adjust. Henry had to become accustomed to the comfort of warmth and the discomfort of a soft bed; to a nighttime unbroken by moans and snores and the pot's stench; to the freedom of being able to sing, talk, open doors; to having no need to hoard tid-bits inside his shirt or put out a cigarette savingly when it was smoked halfway through.

For Johnny, who as a minor had not been allowed

prison visits, it was a matter of getting used to the person he hadn't seen in a child's decade; used to finding the big bedroom door locked; used to no longer being number one about the place.

But settle down the males did, as Molly had assured them they would. Henry stopped wandering from room to room, smoking one cigarette after another, making himself queasy with too much rich food, saying, "It's slop-out time," or, "They'll be starting on the mailbags now," or, "No exercise today, it's pissing down." Johnny stopped resenting it when his father got served first, got all the attention from visitors, and was reluctant to be walked yet again around Stepney and shown off.

So life was normal for everybody once more. There were trips for the three of them: zoo, waxworks, Petticoat Lane. They had good noshes in local caffs. There were evenings in the Coach and Horses, with Henry buying drinks all round, even though he agreed cheerily that the Arnold Cross money wouldn't last for ever.

On that score, although Molly knew better than to suggest to her man that he go straight, she did make murmurs about him getting into something semi-legit, if he felt he had to be active: she would be happy to support him. Henry, committal as a rock, said he was looking around.

Things were also normal in respect of the police. Constables on their beats made a point of looking at Henry knowingly or grimly, and a plain-clothes man accosted him in a milk bar to ask a loud "Keeping your nose clean, Gosport?" Henry smiled through it all because, he said, why make them happy by getting riled?

Business went on at its normal pitch for Molly, as did her relationship with Henry. They loved and fought, laughed and yawned. Their sexual couplings took place in various sites around the house, in a taxi, in the back yard of a pub and in a telephone box. They fell asleep in front of the television set. At a party they rolled about hysterically when a wag impersonated a drunk trying to volunteer for Korea. Molly kicked Henry's shin in the kitchen for saying she was the world's worst cook, which was close to true if his world was Stepney; Henry gave Molly a beaut backhander outside the Coach for looking too long at a new barman.

It was even normal when, one Wednesday, Molly came home to find emptiness where there ought to have been Henry, who had arranged to take her out for a slap-up lunch. Molly, far from astounded, shrugged.

This was because her man had been out of stir over a month now and it was only natural he would be getting restless. His absence could have a hundred motives, from seeing another woman to planning a job. It would all work out. It was all normal.

On arrival in Exeter, Alma was mildly disappointed to find the car park full. On her Wednesdays off she always felt more secure, could enjoy herself more, padded with the knowledge that the Bradford was under a paid eye instead of being left in the street, where that broken doorlock would permit entry to thief or joy-rider.

A full car park had happened to Alma before. All she need do, she knew, was sit and wait. In ten minutes, or one or twenty, somebody would drive out and she could drive in. Wait she could not, being impatient, convinced that by the same law that made a dropped slice of bread land butter-side down nobody would leave the park for at least an hour, simply on account of her lack of patience.

Appreciating this foolishness, which she would have cultivated had she known how, Alma drove on. When she parked it was in as busy a street as she could find with a space available. She walked off and ordered herself not to think about thieves, to think fun.

So first of all, Alma agreed, she would use part of the saved parking fee to buy an ice-cream cone, which she would eat right out in public as she walked along the street, her gloves off.

One way of rendering another person's good fortune acceptable is by shaking the head at what a variety of no good ends it could come to. Wednesdays, ignoring his own Fridays out, Donald's way was to follow that dubious headshake with a list of the treat things he would do instead of labouring away like a coolie; things he later changed his mind about, choosing work, in order to make martyr hay.

Repairing fruit boxes in a shed behind the house, Donald was musing that for lunch he would have beans on toast or some other dish frowned on by Alma. After that he would spend some time with his stamp collection, have a long hot soak, play a bit of Haydn, give a thought to—

There was a shout. Male, it came from somewhere toward the road. Donald cocked his head, the way people do when they want to let themselves know how alert they are right now. The shout sounded again. It came from beyond the house.

Downing tools and going out, Donald supposed the caller to be either a salesman or a private buyer, out of luck both: farm needing nothing, apples sold wholesale only.

He circled to the house frontage, where stood a man.

Oddly, there was no accompanying vehicle. The stranger, about whom hung shreds of the familiar, wore a spiv suit, a side-cocked hat and the type of dark glasses sported by gangsters in Italian films. He gave one slow nod.

Donald asked, "Did you fly?"

The man said, "Walked from the village." His voice was gruff, his accent cockney.

"Good for you."

"You alone?"

"What?"

"The little lady."

Donald frowned, feeling uncomfortable. He said, "If you mean my wife, she's out. There's nothing she wants anyway, whatever you happen to be selling."

"Not selling nothing, Morgan," the stranger said.

"Oh?"

"Nothing."

It was then that recognition took Donald by the lungs. What had fooled him before wasn't the facial camouflage of sunglasses and hat, it was the way Henry Gosport stood, a feet-spread chin-up jauntiness so different from the stance he had adopted in the Old Bailey dock.

"Look," Donald said.

"Yeah?"

Donald heard himself start to talk at nervous speed, culprit lies. Quietly appalled he listened to a toadying, trashy mention of duty done, debts paid to society, a bright future, honesty being the best policy. He asked a breathless:

"Looking for work, eh?"

Henry Gosport said, "I think we'll go inside."

"What's that?"

"We're going in the house."

"Look here, old man," Donald said, folding slightly sideways in the clutch of his sincerity. "I can't give you a job but I do have connexions in the district. You leave your phone number. I'll be in touch. I'm sure I can find you something."

"Inside."

"Just give me your number."

"Go in the house."

"See, I don't need to write it down. Tell me and I'll remember. I've got a fantastic memory."

Henry Gosport put a hand inside his jacket. When he drew it out again he held a gun.

The move was so expected, so even hoped for to end his ache of dire anticipation, that Donald said a gentle, "Yes." With a tired feeling of wistfulness he knew he was going to be killed.

This languor of dread ended when Gosport, reducing the space between them to a yard, raised the black automatic and pointed it straight at Donald's face.

Donald experienced terror. He had never known it before. In spirit he felt the way a scream sounds. In body he felt like the screamer.

His breathing, tight ever since recognition had made its grab, became a task of some difficulty, so that he seemed to be using only the uppermost tops of his lungs, which, further, were being abused by a battering from his heart. His knees pained, he wanted to urinate.

Only vaguely was Donald aware of his actions as he cowered down and back, face flinching a grimace, one hand raised to a forward position between his eyes and the gun. His other hand was stretched out behind, reaching. The pose was classic; almost noble; certainly elegant.

Jerking his gun-bearing arm Henry Gosport said, "Inside, Morgan. Move. Come on."

"What you going to do?" Donald asked, reversing, the
words run together on a single gasp.

"You'll see."

"We'll talk."

Barking, a sergeant: "*Inside!*"

Pose obtaining, his arms making a see-saw, Donald led
the way in reverse into the house. He fumbled, stumbled.
In the living room he backed to a wall and said, "Stop it."

"Stop it?"

"If you don't stop pointing that gun at my face I'm
going to be sick." He was surprised at his courage. He felt
an inkling of hope.

His gun lowered to chest-aim, Henry Gosport said,
"You lied about me."

Donald asked, "What d'you want?" His voice was stead-
ier.

"You lied about me in court and I'm going to kill you."

"It was dark."

"I'm going to kill you."

"I couldn't see all that clearly."

"You said I was armed and I wasn't."

"Yes yes, I could've been mistaken," Donald said. His
body had straightened to a stoop. "I'm sorry."

"Thank you very much."

"I mean it."

Henry Gosport said, "I did have a gun on me, matter of
fact, but it never came out of me pocket."

"No, it was Charles Grew that did the murder. You,
I'm sure, were innocent."

"Oh, I wouldn't go that far, mate."

"I'm sorry if I made a mistake," Donald said. "But it's all over now."

"You ever do porridge?"

"What?"

"Been in prison?"

"I was in the glasshouse for three days once."

Henry Gosport shook his head slowly. His manner, as all along, was casual enough to be chilling. Despite that, Donald had lost the thrust of his terror. He was frightened, but settling. While still accepting that his life could be taken from him he felt he had a chance to keep it. He knew he would have to settle a lot more, however, before his mind began to function around the stage at which he could see where that chance lay.

Gosport said, "Prison's not nice."

"I'm sure it isn't," Donald said. "My wife."

"Eh?"

"She'll be back any minute."

"Right, then," Henry Gosport said. "I'd better get on with it." The gun rose.

In a whimper Donald said, "No." He cringed his face aside from the mouth of the barrel. "She won't, she won't."

"Course not. Think I'm stupid."

"Please. I'll be sick."

As the gun sank the telephone rang. Gosport made no move, not even to look around. Donald leaned away from the wall. Instantly feeling weak he leaned back again and asked, "Shall I answer it?"

"No."

"Maybe I ought to."

"Why?"

He shook his head sadly. "I don't know."

Until the call-signal stopped they were silent, Donald wondering unhappily if that had been his chance. Rings gone, Henry Gosport said, "Your evidence."

"Anyone can make a mistake. It was dark."

"You could see dead clear, you said."

"I was confused. Wrong. I can't tell you how sorry I am."

"Fat lot of good that is."

Donald lied, "I would be prepared to make a new statement to the authorities."

"Bit late now," Gosport said.

"No, it's never too late."

"It should've been done when Molly was here."

"Molly?"

"My lady friend. She came to see you."

"I was unwell, that day."

"She wanted help with the Appeal."

"I was sick."

"You're easy sick, Morgan," Henry Gosport said. He let the gun sink as he stepped forward. In a flash of a movement his other arm came up.

Donald cried out. But the blow that sang across his face was light, a slap, contemptuous. It left no pain behind, only a tingle, and that faded fast under the heat of his shame at the way he had given the cry.

Gosport: "Put your arms down."

He was holding his forearms crossed near his head, Donald realised. He brought them midway down with, "Don't hit me."

"I waited a long time to do that."

"Anyone can make a mistake."

"That's true."

"Yes?"

Henry Gosport said, "Put your arms down properly so I can hit you again."

"No."

"All the way down."

"No."

The gun came up, Donald snapped his arms to his sides, he saw that same flash of movement. But this was a punch. It caught him beside the eye with cracking force and spun him around so that his face smashed against the wall.

The idea might never have occurred to her if it hadn't been for Johnny going on and on. The minute he had come in the house from school he had started to poke about and nag.

"I *know* I dint take it out to play," he said for the fifth time, looking behind a chair.

"All right. Take what?"

"Me gun. It's *got* to be here somewhere."

Molly, resigned, she seemed to spend half her life searching for Johnny's lost toys, turned from the stove to ask, "The cowboy one Aunt Millie give you, Christmas?"

"No no no," her son said in derision, for all the world as though she had suggested he might care to take up the violin. "It's me G-Man."

"Flat thing?"

"Yeah. It's me favourite. I coulda swapped it dead easy for a puppy and two rubber daggers."

"Don't you bring no dogs around me. As if I didn't have enough on my plate."

Johnny knelt in front of the sideboard and began to sift among the lurkers beneath. "Bloody thing's got to be somewhere around. I *know* I dint take it out."

"Bet you did," Molly said. "Anyway, don't bother now, come and get this hot pot into you. That's best of brisket in there, that is."

Johnny now grumbling his way into the food after being told to belt up about the frigging G-Man and eat, Molly got her dismal idea in respect of guns and Henry's absence. Could he have gone to do a job?

Unable to wait until she was alone, Molly left table and room, went into the front parlour, carefully closed the door. Behind a heavy-framed picture, which she swung out from the wall on hinges, was a safe. Ignoring that, she slid up the picture's back of plywood, opening a hiding place that a dozen police searches over the years had failed to discover. In it, as usual, were four guns. Molly blew a whistle of relief.

Grunting with effort, Donald pushed up to arm's-length from where he had been stretched flat on the polished boards that surrounded the carpet. His dizziness had cleared. Beneath him he saw blood and pieces of china. The lightweight table he had brushed against in falling had overturned, breaking the ornament it supported.

To see if he was right in thinking there would also be blood on the wallpaper, Donald turned his head quickly. Right he was. Failing to acknowledge the absurdity in his passing fret over what Alma was going to say, he pushed on up to a tall kneel and lifted both hands to his face, which felt numb.

"We got ourselves a little nosebleed," Henry Gosport said in a croon. "Dear me."

"I hit it on the wall," Donald said as candidly as though

an explanation were called for. His tone was a cross between excuse and apology.

"You poor thing."

"Yes."

"Sure you're not going to faint?"

"I'm all right."

Gosport, who stood nearby, gun alert if not aimed, said in a normal voice, "See, I want your attention."

"Okay."

"You real sure I got it?"

Donald nodded elaborately while bringing out a handkerchief. He realised he felt better than he had felt before the punch, which oddness he discovered to be an additional assurance, prize for winning a prize.

Henry Gosport: "I want to be sure you understand."

"What about?"

"Me killing you."

Dabbing his nose Donald said, "I see." After every dab he looked at the red blots on his handkerchief, not without genuine interest.

"You think I'm killing you out of spite, Morgan, I know. Well, I'm not."

"Would you like a cup of tea?"

"I'm killing you cos it's deserved," Henry Gosport said. He hefted his gun in rhythmic swings.

In the middle of telling himself what you had to do was keep them talking, Donald thought of his service revolver. It was in the attic. Out of an unconscious desire to keep the thought hidden, he gave a distracting cough. He felt shrewd without knowing why, yet did know his chance was swelling.

Henry Gosport: "You *deserve* to be killed."

Donald, nose dry, put his handkerchief away. He wondered how he looked. He said, "Ah."

"I don't spect you to agree with me."

"No."

"But that's the reason."

With his eyes averted from Gosport, Donald pointed out inside that all he had to do was get upstairs to his desk. The revolver was in the drawer. It wasn't loaded but the bullets were there as well, lying around. Dozens of bullets.

Made to feel better still by that last fact Donald said, "I'm not sure I understand you."

"Look," Henry Gosport said. "Your lies could've got me topped. That would've made you guilty of murder."

"There was no danger of you being executed."

"Don't argue with me."

"Sorry."

"I'll kick your head in."

"Very sorry."

"You was trying to commit murder," Gosport said. "It was deliberate. With me, it was different. It was what they calls spur of the moment."

"With you?"

"Right."

"When?"

"The robbery."

"You didn't kill Cross."

Henry Gosport said, "I know. Charlie did. It wasn't necessary. Job was a walkover. The idiot. I was so pissed off about that, I jabbed him one with the sword. I was fit to be tied." He ballooned his cheeks and then emptied them of air with an outslurp.

Weakly, Donald sat back on his heels. "He was your friend. You stabbed your friend?"

"Lovely friend. Mad as a hatter. Turns a clean simple job into a murder case."

"My God."

"Arnold Cross saw him with a gun and me holding that bleeding sword, and listen, he wasn't about to offer no arguments. He would've give us *ten* briefcases."

"But you did try to help him. Grew."

"Got the idiot away from there, yes. Didn't want him narking on me, did I, if he was going to get better. But he was safely on the way out."

With a slow rub of his thighs Donald warned himself he had to be careful. He had to be crafty. He had to use every bit of his brain if he wanted to live.

"So I was all right," Henry Gosport said. "And at the finish I had a genius for a barrister. Expensive but a genius. I haven't finished paying him yet."

"Money," Donald said suddenly.

"With anyone else I would've been lucky to get five years. If the likes of you'd had your way I would've got the rope or life. Lovely. Beautiful."

"You still could, if you kill me. If they catch you for it. And they will. They always do. Killing me won't do you any good anyway. Money will."

"Money?"

"What you need is a start. New life. Pastures."

"What you on about, Morgan?"

Mini-bouncing his clasped hands Donald said, "I've got some money. It's upstairs. It's not a lot but it could give you a start in the world. That's all you need. A bit of cash." He paused. "Eh?"

"I dint say nothing."

"Be real useful, a bit of money. I've got it upstairs. We could go and get it."

Henry Gosport put his head on one side. "I reckon you do owe me something."

"That's the way."

"How much you got?"

"We'll have to see," Donald said, his voice as light as though talking to a child about what will happen if it's as good as could be. His heart was thudding again but not with fear, with the excitement of a possible victory.

Gosport asked, "I mean, a lot or just a few quid?"

"We'll have a look. Come on."

"Be careful."

"I know," Donald said. He got stiffly to his feet. "I'm not going to try anything."

"It's your lookout if you do. Go on."

Leading the way to the stairs, Donald knew it to be without importance that beyond petty cash, a few shillings, he had no money, in his den or anywhere else, including the bank, since even if he did have there would be no change in the murderous intentions of Henry Gosport, who merely wanted whatever was gettable before he pulled the trigger, and who therefore had to be killed.

Donald turned onto the staircase. "Up we go."

"Nice and steady," Henry Gosport said, following. "We don't want no accidents, do we?"

"No, we don't."

"Good."

As he climbed Donald was agreeing with himself that once they were in the attic he would act without delay. He would distract Gosport's attention long enough to get close and give him a mighty shove, if not actually manage to knock the automatic out of his hand. Then he would dash to his desk, get the revolver and a bullet, load quickly—and shoot. He wouldn't have to hesitate. The man was a self-confessed murderer.

They went onto the landing and along it, started up the second flight. Henry Gosport came at the plod of a forty-year-old cigarette smoker, which increased Donald's growing sensation of superiority.

They came to the top. The room into which Donald led the way was long and jumble-crammed under a sloped ceiling. He drew to a halt midway to his desk. Quickly his mind was trying out phrases: *Look at that, Ever see one of those, Know what this is.*

Henry Gosport had stopped across the threshold, two yards distant. He was looking around. Both his arms were down straight. After fixing his attention on a model aeroplane he shifted it up to a kite hung at the roof apex.

"I had a kite once," he said.

"They're fun."

"It got away."

Donald began to back off.

Henry Gosport took no notice.

Donald went on backing. His rump touched the desk, he shifted sideways. He moved in reverse again at the corner. At the desk's rear corner he stopped.

"String broke and it got away."

Finally taking his eyes off Gosport, Donald leaned down. He started to pull open the drawer. It made no noise. He stopped when there was enough open. The revolver lay there among oddments and rubbish.

Henry Gosport asked, "Where's the tent?"

Looking up, tense: "What?"

"Molly said there was a tent."

"Put away. That was a long time ago."

"Over a year," Gosport said with meaning. Taking off his dark glasses he bent forward to peer toward a stuffed owl. He was standing in profile.

Donald sat in his chair fronting the drawer. Working by touch he reached inside and clasped the gun. He delicately lifted it out and beneath the drawer, where it was out of sight. He put it in his left hand. Reaching in again he scuffled softly about in search of a bullet. Throughout all this he had kept, still kept, his wide tight eyes fixed on the other man and his mouth in a smile.

Henry Gosport glanced aside from the owl. "You stuff this thing yourself?"

Donald held all movement. "Yes." Once started on the try at taxidermy he had refused to give in. It had taken months to finish. He twitched his shoulders. "Yes."

"It's a eagle, right?"

"Right."

Gosport looked away again. "Pongs a bit."

"Age," Donald said through his smile in going back on the furtive search.

"Ugly, too."

The smile faded during the time it took Donald to locate by touch and bring out a bullet, fumble it unseen into a chamber and silently move the cylinder around to the position for firing. He was ready.

Henry Gosport was losing interest in the owl.

Taut, not quite believing what was happening, Donald raised the revolver into view. He pointed it and stretched his arm out. Aiming for the heart, he pulled the trigger as Gosport was turning toward him.

They both gasped at the explosion. While the recoil was lifting Donald's arm in the air, Henry Gosport was bursting backwards. His face was a silliness. He crashed to the floor. His limbs settled. He lay still.

If there was one thing the British didn't mind it was queuing, Alma thought, mostly to convince herself she didn't mind standing here in the restaurant, five or six back from the front. The reason they didn't, however, had nothing to do with fortitude or any level remotely connected to the noble, but was because after a decade of war and post-war, years of rationing, shortage and austerity, a queue was the nation's most familiar sight and queuing its most common activity. The docile file had become a part of everybody's daily life. It existed even at the rear door of shops that did extra trade in the black market. There was no trick of place-jumping and front-joining unknown about, no subterfuge of feigned pregnancy or madness or dotage unseeable through. People stood in line for everything from candles to the visas that would take them away to a land without queues.

Convinced, Alma shifted her weight onto the other leg and drew deeply of the restaurant's fragrance: cakes, gravy, cork-tipped cigarettes and Indian carpet. It was the best yet of the morning's samples, in Marks & Spencer, the shoe store, the flower market, the Kardomah frontage.

For not having surrendered to the call of that last voluptuous perfume, surged in to buy a pound of coffee, Alma was proud of her steel. As elsewise this morning, including the ice cream, she had stuck with her decision to spend nothing, just browse and sniff. There were few things more gratifying, more soul-soothing, than preceding a matinee with lunch in a nice restaurant. Sandwiches you could have any old time. Those in the van she would give to a stray dog.

Pleased with that thought, which was why she had repeated it, Alma looked about her at the others waiting for tables, all of them female.

Furthermore queues were marvellously democratic, she mused. Where your average Anglo-Saxon type would decline to address a stranger in any other public place, in queues it was not only done, it was expected to be done.

Everyone conversed, Alma pursued. As well as helping to pass the wait away, it stated that you were all in the same boat, on the same side, comrades. If there was one thing that made the British seem human, it was a queue.

The women ahead of Alma were chatting busily about flower arranging and their club. Of the trio behind, two were whispering together while the other appeared to be bored, face sleepy, though she looked away with a stab of indifference when Alma, having roused the courage, cleared her throat at her. Alma went back to savouring the fragrance.

Between the extremes of ugliness and beauty, the plainest of all a disaster's many faces is the despondency of those who were not in it; the prettiest is a survivor's shining conviction that he has done something clever.

The way Donald felt was a greatly magnified version of his punch aftermath. Having dropped back into his chair following the shot, he sat amid the stink of gunfire growing steadily more enthroned.

Repeatedly, between upcraning looks over the desk at his motionless enemy, Donald gazed around the room with an increasing lack of astonishment, long-shot winner believing. He knew Henry Gosport was dead and Donald Morgan lived on, the Donald Morgan who was one of those quiet fellows you would think couldn't say boo to the picture of an elephant but who could rise to power when the occasion demanded it. This particular quiet fellow had bested a vicious gangster.

Donald imagined how the police would look at him from behind their awe, heard the flattering things they would be forced to say despite their envy.

He reckoned that in all probability they would refer to the fact that at Gosport's trial he had modestly declined to be called a hero. They would do so with those appreciative sways to the side.

Don't go on sitting there, telephone the police station in Cranwell, Donald ordered with authority, a voice of reason prevailing over the coziness.

Not without regret, he put his revolver down. He looked at it for a moment after he had risen, liking the view, wishing suddenly that he had a photograph of the moment when he had fired. He circled his desk, stopped, gave another order: Check to see if he's really dead.

With the faintest of worries Donald went to the supine form. Getting down on one knee he felt for a wrist pulse. He could find nothing. That wasn't proof enough. But he didn't care to feel for a beat at the heart because there was a wound behind that new hole in the jacket and there would be no sense in him lifting an eyelid since he didn't know what to look for.

Donald had risen, his intention being to go and find a small mirror to hold in front of the mouth, see if it clouded with breath, when he recalled what he had once seen a medic do at a shooting-range accident. From the drawer he fetched a pin. He jabbed it into the flesh directly under a fingernail; squeezed; produced no blood.

Henry Gosport was decidedly dead.

His gun, on the floor, was close. In looking at it in time

with a warning not to touch it, fingerprints, Donald noted the silvery scratches.

He averted his eyes quickly, looked back at leisure. With a smile for the foolishness of the idea which sneaked into his mind he leaned across Gosport for a closer look. The truth he saw at once. The gun was a toy.

Donald snatched it up. His smile trying to stay, he turned the black-painted object over and around close to his eyes as he battered home his knowledge that what he held was a lightweight alloy imitation of an automatic pistol and not a particularly good one at that.

Old man finished weeding, Donald got up. After throwing the toy down onto its dead owner with a petulant armswing, he turned and left the room. He plodded downstairs. He didn't know where he was going.

First, when Donald eased off on being shocked and offended, cheated, he set about explaining to himself how natural it was that he should have been taken in.

The subdued lighting indoors made for poor observation (that he had been outdoors on the weapon's first appearance he forgot). The gun had been some distance away. Most of it had been hidden inside Gosport's big lower-class fist. It had been aimed not by a child, in fun, but by a man known to be a gangster and confessedly a murderer, in earnest. Anyone would have been fooled. Anybody in the world.

The explanation sputtered. Donald was starting to see a completely different police reaction to his victory. It made him sweat on his neck.

He had killed an unarmed man.

There was only his own word that Henry Gosport had held on him what seemed to be a gun.

There was only his own word that Gosport had

brought with him any gun at all. It could be the house-holder's.

There was only his own word that he had been punched in the face by Gosport. Bloody noses and broken ornaments were not all that difficult to arrange.

There was only his own word that Gosport had said he had come to kill him.

So why had he come?—Donald questioned, looking around. He saw he was sitting on his bed. He let himself fall backwards, turned onto his side, curled up small. The question throbbed on like jealousy.

After a while the obvious began to present itself. It took so long to arrive due to needing to break through a thicket of resistance: Donald's reluctance to admit that he had failed to see said obvious.

Henry Gosport came not to kill a goose but to get an understanding on a regular supply of its golden eggs. Extortion, that was his game. If murder had been his plan he would have come by night, unseen, not openly in day-light, by train and on foot, taking a chance on finding his mark both home and alone. The slap, the punch, the threats, the claim of having stabbed Charles Grew, they were to frighten his intended larceny victim into mallea-bility. Gosport wanted an income.

Even if the gangster's automatic had been real, Donald saw, he could still be charged with murder. He would have to prove the automatic wasn't his own. He would also have to explain why he was in illegal possession of a re-volver. That thousands of ex-servicemen had unregistered army-issue or souvenir weapons at home would make no difference.

Donald perked at a twinkling possibility. Could he, he wondered, get away with telling the police Henry Gosport had come armed with the revolver, that they had fought for possession of it and in the struggle it had gone off?

It was a worthy notion, except for the shot not having been fired at close range, but that might be fixable, fake-able. Hopeful, Donald stopped stroking his thumb under his bottom lip—until he realised that probably the re-volver would be traceable to himself through army records.

Before he could fall immediately to gloom again Donald got out the balm. He offered self-praise for his presence of mind following the shooting. Anybody else would have called the police straight off, not waiting to consider the situation from every viewpoint.

But what was there to consider?—Donald thought, fall-ing. There was nothing to weigh up, unless . . .

The unless, he recognised, meant not reporting what had happened. Which meant erasing all traces of Henry Gosport's visit and getting rid of the body.

But was he not, Donald asked, being too dramatic? Was he not seeing this in the worst possible light?

He pictured a sympathetic detective. He was old and wise, had conducted thousands of investigations, owned an instinct about murder that had never steered him wrong.

Don't worry, Mr. Morgan. You've been through a shattering experience and naturally enough your nerves are tattered. Take your time about answering. Respectable citizens like yourself have nothing to fear.

Donald, however, after a friendly start, was unable to prevent the detective's probing from taking the direction which until this moment he hadn't seen himself. He scraped his thumb-nail against his lower teeth.

Was there a criminal connexion between you and Henry Gos-

port? After all, you had been on the scene of the Cross robbery. In court you did your utmost, it looked like, to get Gosport convicted. Maybe that was just to make you seem more uninvolved, maybe to get him hanged so you would have all the proceeds of the armed robbery for yourself. Did Gosport come to settle with you, one way or the other? Did he come for his share? If you're a respectable citizen, why do you keep an unlicenced, unregistered firearm hidden in your house?

Donald got off the bed. In what space was available in the room, he began to pace. Half an hour he spent in going over the whole matter and dead-ended with the conclusion that if the police were brought in he would be charged with a felony.

At best, Donald reckoned, he would be found not guilty, following months in jail and a trial whose expense would drive him into bankruptcy; at worst, if not *the* worst, which didn't bear thinking about, he would be found guilty of manslaughter and sentenced to three years imprisonment.

Contacting the police was therefore out. The body had to be disposed of.

Bedroom left at a stride, Donald went down one flight of stairs, through to the rear of the house and outside. He was heading for a shovel, planning on where to dig, when his gaze fell on the kiln. He halted.

Not everyone considers himself to be above average in intelligence. The figure has been calculated at 97 per cent for women and 99 per cent for men. Alma Morgan was among that 3 per cent of the modest.

Which didn't prevent her from muttering to herself about Lila Wriggley's gross stupidity. Lila, researcher for the Exeter Historical Society, was sitting across the room from the queue's head, presently formed by Alma, who had waved at Lila twice without getting a response.

That all those diners who, rather than get up and leave, were passing time by staring insolently or gloatingly at the queuers had missed seeing the waves go unanswered had not stopped Alma from feeling hot and silly. Nor did Lila Wriggley's preoccupation with her three companions plus the fact of her glasses being steamy-greasy stop Alma's slanderous mutters.

Not that she knew the researcher all that well, was in the habit of sending her waves. But it had made her feel less of a loner to see a familiar face, as well as appear to others to be less of a one, the more important of the two.

Now, in several parts of the restaurant, people were getting organised for leaving. Alma hummed a sigh that her wait was almost over. On noting departure action at the Wriggley table also, she smiled, knowing for sure that the black-clad manageress would come to fetch her before she could say hello to Lila as she passed.

Which happened. Following the woman, Alma did look back with a hand poised in case Lila looked over as she headed for the exit; she didn't. And now it didn't matter.

Alma was left at a table for two. Sitting, she exchanged a simper with the other occupant, a middle-aged woman with a bobbled veil depending from her hat, lipstick on her dentures and a newspaper on her lap.

The woman said, "It's all politics nowadays, isn't it?"

"Oh yes," Alma said with a friendly sway. "The papers talk about nothing else."

"Or strikes."

"Yes, the Unions. They're getting more powerful all the time, aren't they?"

Nodding, the woman went on eating in a crouch, her

eyes on the newspaper. To another comment on organised labour she merely nodded again. Alma picked up
the menu.

When the waitress came at a bustle, breathing of-
fendedly, Alma ordered Windsor soup, Dover sole, apple
crumble. After another try at prising the woman away
from her newspaper, she settled back and told herself how
lovely this was.

Donald, coming at a creep downstairs, in reverse, hated
the way Henry Gosport's feet clumped down from step to
step. They were so loose and heavy, so suggestive of an
idiot cripple. The sound too grim, drumbeat in a
gravebound procession.

Dragging, however, was the only answer. Getting the
body hoisted to a carrying position Donald had found
impossible, at least during the time he gave to the project,
jaw jutted in his refusal to be bested by the inanimate.

Since he wasn't hidden inside paint, putty nose and
baggy clothes in order to stand, or enjoy, being a figure of
fun, Donald had relented as soon as he got the suspicion
that his flop-stumble efforts were beginning to look farci-
cal.

Gosport held under the armpits, Donald turned onto
the landing. As he backed along its carpet he was pleased
to realise he was making a note to take care of the two
scuff lines caused by the heels. He started down the bottom flight. Clumping he abnegated by thinking about his
kiln.

He had built it himself four years ago, with Morgan
Orchards' future looking insipid. Good old-fashioned
earthenware, that was the thing that could be built up
into a going concern, Donald had been convinced. There

were always buyers for your simple crockery, and the clayey soil hereabouts would do nicely, thank you, as well as being free.

Bricks for the shoulder-tall five-by-five oven Donald had salvaged from a tip, the iron door he bought had once been on a ship's boiler, gas lines came from a junk-yard.

That he had fired his kiln but three times, not enough to refine the crockery making, learn how to eliminate cracks, he, in apple blossom time, had felt to be unimportant when measured against the fun and excitement of construction. Furthermore, it would always be there to fall back on.

He was sometimes, in a quiet way, prophetic, Donald thought in coming off the staircase. There was much more to him altogether than people divined.

Crouching with the weight, he dragged on outdoors at the back, past a shed and to the kiln, where he let Gosport drop. Breath recovered, he searched pockets, his eyes everywhere except on the dead face. Personal papers and return train ticket he left, money he took, as he already had sunglasses, wristwatch and toy automatic.

Getting Gosport through the thirty-inch-square door-frame at hip level was easier than expected, making Donald blink toughly. He closed the door, lit the gas.

Turning away with a symbolic double slap-off of the hands, which he couldn't resist doing, Donald thought, That gets shut of the corpus delicti.

The Latin term came back to him repeatedly while he was in a shed, at its workbench, battering to pieces the dark glasses, toy gun and wristwatch; while concurrently musing how much easier, thoroughness apart, the kiln method was than digging a pit; while assuring himself that all traces of his visitor would be gone (the hat was in a pocket) when later he had beaten the bones to powder; while agreeing that his story for Alma in respect of the broken vase, bloodstains and facial damage should be simple; while accepting without rancour the harped reminder to air out his den.

The echo of corpus delicti was because he had used it with Alma a year and a bit ago, Donald recognised finally. Wearing a plump smile of accomplishment, idiot dies for flag, he mused on what had occasioned the term as he tossed scraps of metal and glass into various waste-bins.

Demolition done, Donald, his face straight, thought of the scheme he had dreamed up to form a blow against capital punishment. The situation in which he was presently involved appeared to be perfectly suited. In fact, it was even better in respect of the murder victim's remains. There would be a skeleton, at least, and the bones of Henry Gosport would easily pass for those of Donald Morgan.

He wandered out of the shed. In the minutes it took him to go indoors and flop into an armchair after circling the room, Donald five times told himself not to be a raving lunatic and five times to give it a bloody good think, he might be onto something here.

He thought.

The scheme he considered from many angles, not disregarding his own lack of the identifying dental work which would not be findable on the victim skull.

What Donald was unable to see was the reason he found his plagiarised scheme so attractive: it would mean striking off the suspect list Donald Morgan, the man who just might be responsible for Henry Gosport's disappearance, and thus the subject of revenge by his gangland friends.

Shuffling himself comfortable, Donald played it through. First of all, he detailed, the police would come in answer to an anonymous telephone call. Alma would let them in but be nervous. It would be poor, her explanation for the blood that had been inefficiently cleaned from wall and floor. She would try to divert attention from the kiln and drag marks leading to it, which, followed back, would lead to the attic, where a smell of gunfire lingered. The police would nose about all over the place. Findable would be the revolver and the pieces of ornament, and, of course, the victim's remains.

Maybe Alma could even confess straight off, Donald thought as he crossed his legs and folded his arms, a double cuddle. Either way she would be arrested. She would be tried for murder. They would have to find her guilty. And, it was hoped, she would be sentenced to death.

Then the supposed victim would appear.

Sensation.

Donald tightened the clench of his arms and legs. He had a tingle of excitement. He was seeing not so much the blow against judicial homicide as the sudden, great, beautiful fame of Donald Morgan. He saw it with the clarity and sweetness of a favourite dream. He saw it at considerable length.

Presently, leaning forward in the chair uncuddled, Donald once more went through the whole idea, stroking it here, adding there a touch of sophistication, discarding the crass and the flagrant, overall sculpting with a finesse to make his continuing excitement seem understated.

The question of how he would later post-sensation explain the bones made no appearance until he had found an answer. It was simple. He could say he had dug the skeleton up a couple of years ago; with it were fragments of newsprint that dated from the late 1800s; exposed to the air, they had soon disintegrated.

This, however, led to Donald realising that, come whatever, he could not tell his wife the truth. She, naively believing all would be well, would insist on reporting the death of Henry Gosport to the authorities, which he couldn't possibly do as he had no explanation of why he had destroyed the body.

To Donald, the scheme began to look not only attractive, but necessary, a combination with the potency of beauty and brains. He went to make a cup of tea, over the ceremony of which he hoped to come to a decision.

Could it be she had said something wrong to the newspaper reader? A remark about the Unions that had been misconstrued? Or had it been the way she had looked at that awful veil, with its antiquated bobbles, the look giving offence?

As soon as she had left the table, mumbling "Good day," the only thing she had said since their initial exchange, Alma had started obsessing about the woman. She had ended it by making plain to herself both that she was thinking this way as a substitute for conversation, which traditionally went with meals, and that the poor woman could have hundreds of reasons for not being gregarious, from deafness or illness to worry or love.

Now moving aside her plate, on which not a trace of apple crumble remained, Alma expertly caught the attention of her waitress by using a prominent gape. Plodding across the near-empty restaurant, her lacy apron soiled and sad, the girl teetered beside the table to write out the bill.

Compassionately, Alma said, "You do work hard here, you girls, I'll say that for you."

"Yes'm," the waitress said, alert as a hole. She put the slip of paper down and left on, "Thank you."

The bill had vegetable instead of Windsor, Alma noted. The restaurant was being cheated out of sixpence. Should she call the girl back from where she was sagged with others by the kitchen door? Of course not.

Sliding a sixpence and a shilling under the plate, Alma got up. She went to the counter. It was unattended. She put down the right amount on top of the bill and left.

Outside, Alma began to stroll. Her gloves she left off for the cheek of it. She hummed. The cinema was two streets away and she wished it were ten; wished, suddenly, that she were on the crest of a vast meadow with nothing to see but sky and distance.

To mock her discomfort at this foolishness while privately admitting it had every right to exist, Alma laughed —before ticking off that she ought to be ashamed of herself for having suchlike notions.

Savingly, however, Alma felt sure that if she were out in the romantic wilds she would be self-chiding for having reveries about strolling in town, full of good food, heading for a matinee. She hoped it would be a damned good weepy.

At the cinema Alma bought her ticket and passed into the waiting auditorium, where Bing Crosby and the Andrews Sisters were giving their all through the sound system.

Graciously Alma indicated to an usherette that she would find her own place, which she did, an isolated spot among the scattering of moviegoers, after a thorough look around and a surreptitious ridding of her ticket stub. She sat with a sigh, pampered to a nicety.

Donald Morgan was one of those people who, not liking to be rushed, sold, pressured, can resist the finest line of patter. This Donald devoutly believed. Despite having bought a dubious bill of goods more often than your average gull, he was convinced far past the penumbra of a doubt, knew, that no salesman had ever managed to sell him something which he himself hadn't wished to buy in the first place.

What Donald did not know was that the greatest salesman of all those he had met in his life, losingly, was himself—when the customer was Donald Morgan.

By the time he had finished his cup of tea he had signed on the dotted line, with a flourish. He had decided. It was full speed ahead. His scheme was on.

One of the more telling clinchers had been the last. It wasn't everyone who got the chance to change judicial history, Donald allowed. In time they might call it the Morgan Act. Perhaps in longer time, when the Establishment had cooled down, there would be a knighthood.

Donald walked briskly out of the kitchen. There was a lot to get organised.

It was in turning his mind in mild embarrassment from tasting "Sir Donald" that he remembered he had recently killed someone, a man who had been playing a non-lethal game; and it was in swinging away from that awkwardness to thoughts of Alma that he recognised a barrier.

He stopped, wheeled around, went back into the kitchen. After a spate of directing his eyes blindly out of

the window, he sat by his cup at the table. He had intimations of despondency.

Even without knowing anything about Henry Gosport's death, Donald had to see, Alma could still easily
refuse to go along with the plan. She could say, and probably would, "Another of your wild ideas, darling? You
can't be serious."

Which caused Donald to realise that, face to face, his
wife would know he was lying—about what had gone into
the kiln, about how the blood had got on the floor and
wall, about everything. Somehow she could always tell
when he was keeping something back or distorting.

His acknowledgement that this was not a rare gift of
Alma's but because he happened to be one of the honest
kind who couldn't lie for the life of them, didn't make
Donald feel any better. Nothing could. He had become
married to the scheme. Having thought it through yet
again while playing salesman, he had found it to be truly
beautiful and brilliant, quite without fault. Did this mean
divorce?

It would seem so.

Before Donald could get into the full wash of a de-
spond, with depression the next wave, even before the
hand of dreariness he started to lift reached his brow, he
had seen the way out. It was obvious, he thought before
changing that to damn clever.

He would set everything up and then go away. Alma he
would telephone the second she got home. There would
be nothing she could do about the situation, except play
along, which, certainly, she would do with pleasure so
long as she thought it was all straightforward—no violence, no Gosport.

Donald became brisk again. He stood up, took a turn around the table, patted himself and laughed.

He nodded. Released from having to face his wife and her penetrating old-fashioned looks, he felt better than ever about what he was going to do. He felt ten years old.

Leaving the kitchen Donald strode to the stairs. As he went up the two flights and along the landing between he was careful not to step on, smooth out, any of the scuff marks. Indeed, at one place he stopped to make a mark deeper.

In his den Donald set about arranging his disappearance.

Out of the jumbled collection of effects on shelves and in corners he selected various items, his lips pursed to show his concentration: a sleeping bag, a pup tent, a knapsack, aluminum cooking utensils, general campsite needs. The absence of these items would not be noticed.

On examination, the tent proved to have a rip. There were two other tents, which, investigated, were worse, one with a longer rip, the third having leaks in its blow-up posts. Donald set to work on the first with needle and thread. He had plenty of time.

The idea for his disappearance Donald considered a stroke of genius. Far from skulking in some obscure boarding house or a cave or the cellar of an abandoned house, he would hide in full view. Wearing hiking gear and toting a knapsack, he would wend the open highways and byways, camping out, until it was time to make his dramatic return to life.

As to the mundane details, Donald would mostly do his own cooking, with the infrequent milk bar snack. Laundry would be the weekly couple of garments. For expenses, initially he had Henry Gosport's money and Morgan Orchards' petty cash, later he would sell some of his postage stamps, a selection from his album taken along. A stroke of pure genius.

Midway through his tent repairing Donald broke off to deal with other, less tedious matters. He brought upstairs a bucket of water, carried carefully to avoid spillage, and into it fired five bullets. He retrieved them when he had taken the bucket down again and, braving its heat, tossed them into the kiln. Six lead blobs would be there for detectives to thrill over.

Coming back up, pleased with the revitalised stink of gunfire, Donald collected revolver and shellcases, which he took down and outside. His not having taken them with him on the last trip had been deliberate: every step of the scene-setting was being savoured.

With a shovel Donald went to a patch of garden not far from the house. He dug two feet down, dropped in revolver plus shells and covered them thinly, leaving the pile of updug soil almost untouched. Shovel he let fall nearby.

He returned to his stitching.

When next Donald came down to the ground floor he was ready for departure. He wore hat, shirt, short pants and socks in khaki, shoes of brown, which items, like their campsite colleagues, would not be missed by Alma, who was not going to be told about the stroke of genius.

Donald accepted that if his wife knew where or how he could be found, she might, being in the wrong mood to fall in with the scheme, or inclined to fall out with it later, inform the authorities where to pick up the supposed murder victim.

With the loaded knapsack on his back Donald made a final tour of the scene. His features were unsteady with contained excitement, his legs with an eagerness to be gone.

Satisfied, Donald left the back way and headed through apple trees. His first hike, overland, all roads avoided for the moment, would take him to a junction where stood a telephone box. He would hide there until Alma drove by, going home. Then he would make a phone call to set his mammoth scheme in motion.

"This is good-bye, Ingrid."

"Yes, my dear."

"I shan't come back. That would be cruel."

"If only we could kiss."

"We can't, they're watching. Smile, darling."

"I am. See how I smile."

"Good-bye."

"Good-bye, my love."

The train moved away. As it began to recede, the girl standing in the foreground with her arm raised, the music swelled and large letters told THE END.

Where greedy is what others call a man who calls himself careful, Alma thought of herself as sentimental where others would have said sloppy. She could have offered no argument as she shuffled up the aisle, using her gloves for a final wipe because her handkerchief was sodden.

When the reason for it will be forgotten in ten minutes, Alma reflected in gratitude, there was no emotional treat as rich as a good weep, unless it was an unqualified scream. Although, it wasn't the acts themselves so much as the following composure. In it you could be remarkably tolerant—except of light.

Cringing her outraged eyes from the afternoon's glare Alma came out of the cinema, one of fifty shifty-mouthed petty thieves whose gloat over having stolen three hours of escape was starting to stale. Along with a tinge of the wretched she felt nicely illicit. She had no problem reading reproach into the glances of passers-by.

Around the next corner Alma saw Mr. Smith approaching. He was that old charmer who ran the ironmonger's in Cranwell and she wouldn't for the world have had him see her red-eyed and blotchy.

There were several shop doorways handy. Into one of them Alma slipped. She stayed there, face averted, until from the edge of her vision she saw Mr. Smith go safely by. She went on.

At the van, Alma took out her sandwiches, one of tomato and one of corned beef. She set off walking.

After ten minutes spent in search of a stray dog, then a dog of any nature, or a cat or a tramp, Alma put the food down unwrapped in an alley, not without a glitter of guilt in respect of the famine-stricken.

She went back to the van and drove away. In twenty minutes as the crow counts she would be home, she mused. For tea she would prepare something scrumptious and, in fact, in pattern, make a fuss of Donald generally. It substituted for his inability to understand, like most men, that no matter how much a woman loved her husband, and love Donald Alma did, she still needed to get away from him once in a frequent while.

There had been a stage when Donald had nearly changed his mind, for if deeds speak louder than words, belches can shout down intentions.

With an hour to go before Alma could be expected to appear, Donald had been like the boy who, having run away from home, begins to feel regret, assailed not by doubt in his wisdom but hunger.

Hiding in bushes on the telephone corner of the crossroads, a quiet junction, Donald had listened to the rumbled carping of his belly. He had missed out lunch. All he had brought to eat in the knapsack was a tin of beans. Furthermore his bare legs were beginning to feel chilled. He yawned. There was a dull climate of anti-climax.

Therefore Donald had given serious consideration to a change of mind. He reckoned he could be back home and have everything arranged long before the return of Alma, who, as usual, would make a delicious meal by way of showing thanks for his liberal attitude toward her days off. She was a fine cook, Alma was. A real talent in the kitchen, in fact.

However: looking about him in an incredulous way at his alien surroundings had served to remind Donald of the semi-recognised: this very foreignness, this escape from the everyday, formed one of his reasons for going along with the scheme. Was he about to throw in the towel out of a little discomfort?

The answer was no.

Seeing that it would, in any case, be dark in less than two hours, Donald had decided to pitch camp. His tent he put up farther back in the bushes, unseeable from the road, to which he meanwhile kept his hearing tuned, familiar as he was with the Bradford van's pom-pom-pom.

After that Donald had made a small fire, warmed up and eaten his beans, put on a raincoat, revelled with shoulder-shivers in the marvel of it all and forgot entirely that he had ever considered cancelling.

Now, not trusting mere hearing in the less sporadic

traffic of evening, Donald was again crouched in the bushes a rock's toss from the telephone box.

Far off he caught the right sound. He waited for volume, peered out and saw his wife go jauntily by. That her appearance was hardly due to any skilled planning on his own part failed to prevent him from feeling smart.

Cautiously Donald rose until he was looking over the bushes. This was a sticky bit, he knew. It wouldn't do to be seen by anyone he was known to, a person who could say afterwards that Donald Morgan had been alive at such and such a time.

Raincoat collar up, hat brim down all round, Donald hurried over to the telephone box and inside. Settled, he dialled the village police station, a three-man operation of two constables and a sergeant. It was the last who answered.

Pitching his voice as high as surprise Donald said, "Look, I'm going to make a report but I don't want to give my name."

"Why not?"

"I don't want to get involved like. It's none of my business after all. But I finally decided I ought to report what I heard out at Morgan Orchards there."

"I know the place," the sergeant said easily. "What's all this about?"

Donald said, "No idea. I stopped by and overheard a real terrible argument. Never heard nothing like it. Mr. and Mrs. Morgan, it was. There was screams, language, crashes. All that."

"Go on."

"Well, there was another crash and I heard Morgan say he was hurt. I heard Mrs. Morgan say that was nothing, she was going to kill him. Then there was running sounds, going upstairs like. Next from the top of the house there was shots. Five or six shots. After that it was dead silent. That's when I left. I thought I ought to make a report." He put the receiver down.

THREE

Nice to be home all the same, Alma informed herself politely as she steered into the doorless wooden garage that was starting to sag sideways. She got out, crossed the frontage, went in the house the front way.

"Dar-ling?" she called out in her two-tone manner. "I'm back again. Dar-ling?"

As she walked into the living room the telephone began to ring. She changed course.

"Darling?"

Even if Alma had been fully aware of getting no answer she would have made weak mental comment, knowing her husband could be anywhere on the property.

At the telephone's small table, one of six they had got at a bargain price, she lifted the receiver. "Morgan Orchards."

"Good afternoon," a male voice said. "I'd like to speak to Mr. Morgan, please."

"Certainly. Who's calling, please?"

There was a pause, at which Alma raised her eyebrows, before the voice asked, "Am I addressing Mrs. Morgan?"

"Yes, you are. Who's calling?"

After another pause, at which the eyebrows came down deep: "This is Sergeant Warner. At the Cranwell station."

"Oh, it's you, sergeant. Hello. How're you?"

"I'm fine, Mrs. Morgan, thank you. Is everything all right over there?"

"Why yes," Alma said, her frown going at this oddness. "Perfectly all right."

"No problems?"

"Not one, no."

"That's good," the policeman said. "Well, could I have a word with Mr. Morgan, please."

"Of course," Alma said. "Hold on a sec." She covered the mouthpiece to call her husband's name, twice. There was no answer. Hand off she said, "He doesn't seem to be in the house, sergeant."

"Oh?"

"I just came in myself. Been in Exeter."

"Oh, have you?"

"Tell you what, sergeant, I'll scout him out wherever he is and ask him to give you a ring."

The sergeant said, "Fine—if you can make it quick." The line clicked off.

Alma frowned again, now at the policeman's peremptory closing attitude, which also made her drop the receiver into its cradle from a height of several inches with a follow of wriggled fingers. Enjoying her satisfaction she turned away, took two steps, stopped in a lean.

Straightening slowly, heavy with the weight of uneasiness, Alma stared at an overturned table, shattered vase, glisten on the boards, dark patch on the wallpaper. Repeatedly her eyes moved from one zone to another.

Not looking away she called, "Donald?"

The lack of answer was so like a silently approaching

attack, she winced. Louder she called out a one-tone "Darling?"

The telephone rang.

Reversing to it Alma fumbled the receiver up and to her face. She heard, "Is that you?"

"Donald."

"The line was engaged."

"It was the police," Alma said dully. "Warner from the village. He wanted to talk to you."

"Thought that might happen."

"You have to call him."

"It doesn't matter," Donald said.

"Yes, he sounded urgent."

"Forget it."

"Darling, there's something wrong."

"No, dear, it's the other way round. Something's right. I'll give you the gen."

Less dull, tightening, Alma said, "You're upset, Don. I can tell. Your voice."

"Not upset—excited. This is big."

"Something's happened here. I'm looking at it now. I think there's blood. I know there is."

Donald said, "Yes, it's mine."

"Oh God. Where are you?"

"Halfway to Birmingham."

"What? Please be serious."

"I am being. I started hitch-hiking as soon as I left the house and I got a lift straight away."

Alma said, "I don't know what's wrong with me. I can't seem to make sense of anything you say. Where *are* you?"

"A hundred miles away," Donald said. "Never mind that for the moment. Let me get you filled in on what's been happening. Right? Right?"

"Yes, darling. Sorry. I suppose I'm being terribly dense, aren't I?"

"No no no."

"Are you hurt? This blood."

"My face is a bit swollen and my nose is sore. It's nothing. But let me tell you."

"Are you in trouble with the police?"

Plodding it: "No I am not."

"Sorry," Alma said.

"Will you listen?"

"Yes, darling."

"Okay," Donald said, his voice taking on a lilt. "Well, it all began when I found the skeleton a few months ago. It gave me an idea. You remember that plot we talked about against capital punishment? Well, here we go."

Staring into space Alma said, "Wait."

"I've been planning it for ages but I didn't do anything until today, after I'd slipped on the boards and fell on—"

"Wait, Donald. Please wait. What skeleton? Is this a practical joke?"

"No, Alma, it isn't."

"Darling, I'm worried."

She would no longer be when he had finished explaining, if he was allowed to, Donald said in the heavy, spaced manner he used instead of a rant. Patient, holding up a hand, Alma told him to carry on.

She was still being patient when finally she started to believe what her husband was saying, accept that he had set up this astounding situation, had done so without so much as a word to her about it, and had now thrust the whole thing into her lap.

Donald asked, "Clear?"

"Darling," Alma said, voice steady to calm them both.

"We can't. Such a venture needs far more planning. What about money? I'd need a lawyer."

"Legal Aid. Everyone's entitled to it. That occurred to me, naturally. I've thought this out, Alma."

"How am I supposed to act? And what about the skeleton? We'll be in trouble if it comes out we're trying to pull a fast one. No, darling, really. I think we should call it off. It's far bigger than you realise."

"Don't be like that," Donald said, knife wrapped in tissue. "The scheme is foolproof. It'll work like a dream. And the goal is wonderful."

"On that I agree, but—"

"Anyway, we can't call it off, the police're in on it already."

Alma said, "I can hardly credit that you called them. That you'd do it before talking to me. Darling. Donald. I don't know what got into you."

"Alma, someone has to do something to stop judicial murder. If we don't, you and I, maybe no one ever will. It's up to us. This is our chance."

"I never knew you felt so strongly about it."

"I do tend to keep these things hidden, I know," Donald said in an offended way.

"It could all turn out badly wrong."

"There's a lot going on inside me that I don't show."

"For instance that blood."

"What about it?"

Alma said, "If I'm supposed to have killed you would I leave the blood there, blatant evidence?" Hearing nothing from the other end she went on, "You see, darling? It hasn't been thought out thoroughly from both sides, ours and theirs. It needs much more time, much more preparation."

"It's too late, Alma," Donald said, emphatic. "They're on their way."

"Who?"

"The police."

"Here? How d'you know?"

From the other end, silence. All this *pausing*, Alma thought, putting a hand on top of her head. When she touched hat, not hair, she suddenly felt ridiculous, which made her feel vulnerable. Gasping faintly she said:

"Come home, Donald. Please do, darling. Stop all this and come back. I'm so alone."

While Donald was saying that the police, obviously, were bound to arrive if he failed to call them at once, there came the sound of a car slowing on the frontage.

Alma slammed the receiver down.

She ran to the kitchen. She snatched up a damp cloth. She ran back to the other room and rubbed at the wallpaper's dark patch. From outside came the closing of car doors. Alma righted the table, footed the broken bits of pottery together by the wall, squatted and wiped at the blood. Its glisten had gone, leaving dullness, by the time a knock sounded.

Alma rose. With a sensation like insanity, the painful wish to snicker, the happy desire to lament, she realised she didn't know what she wanted the police to see, think, do.

She went toward another bout of knocking with the cloth held behind her back, saw that as absurd and ran to the kitchen again. Cloth tossed under sink she set off for the front door, which was rumbling from the abuse of heavier knocking.

Pretending he was still making a call, Donald huddled over the receiver. He had no intentions of leaving the box until there were no sights or sounds of traffic.

While tapping his foot, as a lift, he recalled how clever he had been in not falling into a trap, in not saying he had just seen them go by when Alma had asked him how he knew the police were on their way.

Sporadic traffic went on. Donald grew tense. What, he mused, if one of these drivers needed to make a call, and what if they turned out to be someone who knew him? Bumpingly he left the telephone box with shoulders high.

Reaching the bushes Donald broke into a run. Victory over danger as well as the fast action gave him a charge of exhilaration. He almost felt as though he could take off and fly. He ran faster, head back and mouth wide.

Abruptly, Donald was nearing his tent. The thought hit him fast: Jump it.

His breathing caught with the audacity of his idea plus the splendour of knowing he was a different person now, his life had changed, he was heading for adventure.

Too late to stop, to change course, Donald jumped. It thrilled him into glaring fear and glee above his gaped mouth that everything could be minor spoiled if he came down on the tent and major ruined if he broke a leg.

The four-foot-high apex he cleared with room to spare. He landed heavily but in fair style, not let down by knees long unaccustomed to such harsh treatment. Trotting down to a walk he circled back in hammed elegance, slanting, smiling at his whimsy, the while hoping all would go as successfully at the scheme's other end, that his wife wouldn't fail him.

"I understand," Alma said. She stood facing the two uniformed, helmeted men in the living room. "There's no need to apologise."

There having been no suggestion of apology in his words or mien, the sergeant smiled forgivingly. He was sixty and thin, neck rising scrawny out of his collar, wrists such a mess of sinews that he hid them turn by turn with clasps. He had dark soulful eyes.

"We have to take notice of these anonymous telephone calls whether we like it or not," he said.

In telling herself not to keep glancing toward the pieces of vase, Alma glanced that way twice in quick succession. She asked, "But what happens now? I can't produce my husband. He isn't here."

"Do you know where he is, mum?"

"No."

"Well look, is there any truth in what we was told? Was there an argument and gunfire?"

"What goes on in my house, sergeant, is my own affair," Alma said, admiring what she thought was a good answer. Her confidence was returning. "If, by the way, you would care to remove your helmets, please do so."

"We're all right."

"Good." Her glance toward the shards she swept around to end on the young constable. As several times before, he gave her a nod of reassurance.

Putting his elbows back the sergeant asked, "Do you, Mrs. Morgan, possess a firearm?"

"I? No."

"Well, does your husband?"

"I cannot answer for Mr. Morgan."

"I see."

Alma said, "May I offer you a sherry?"

Elbows normal the sergeant said a morose "We're on duty."

"Or tea. I was just about to make some for myself."

"Tell you what, mum. You make your tea and we'll have a little nose about. Satisfy ourselves."

"Have I the right to say no?"

"You certainly have. Say it and we'll leave."

"Never mind," Alma said. "Nose about all you like. Excuse me." She left and went to the kitchen, where she bustled in putting on the kettle. Her confidence continuing its trudge return from the exile into which it had been sent by Donald's brutality, she was beginning to see that she could do it, go through with the incredible. And hadn't it been her idea in the first place?

Alma wasn't sure about origin, knowing how individual ego could fool people as strongly as the national variety. What mattered was that, shaky though the scheme might be in construction, if it ever became a finished edifice it would have immense power.

Heading for the teapot, Alma saw the wiping cloth. She got it and put it under a running tap. She was looking at the red that came out of her squeeze when the throat was cleared, a piece of theatre that made her want to laugh. Nevertheless she had a serious face to turn with.

Coming in from the doorway Sergeant Warner said, "There's what looks like blood on the wall and floor, Mrs. Morgan. I wonder what that means."

"I have no idea."

"Look. I'm sorry about this, but I think it might be a good idea if you stopped wringing that cloth out."

Promptly, Alma did so. With cloth dropped and tap off she turned again toward the policeman. "It's there when you want it." She reached for a towel.

"Thank you," Warner said. He changed wrist-clasps. "Did you say you'd been out all day, mum?"

"Since about eleven this morning."

"And your husband was here when you left and you don't know where he is now?"

"That is correct."

Into the doorway moved the constable. After giving Alma one of his nods he said mildly, "Sarge, there's drag marks on the carpeting and up in—"

"Hold on, hold on," Warner said. "Just you hold on a bit." He went doorwards with shooing motions and a flipped back "Scuse me, mum." The policemen left.

Though not convinced of its truth, Alma told herself she was beginning to enjoy the situation. All she needed to do for the time being was go on playing a medium game.

She was pouring boiling water into the pot, her hat removed, when Warner came back. Manner unchanged, he said, "There's a smell of shooting in that attic and it looks as if something's been dragged down the stairs."

"Yes?"

"Is there anything you'd like to tell me, Mrs. Morgan, about what happened here?"

"No, thank you."

The telephone rang.

"Excuse me," Alma said, putting the kettle down. Gym mistress leads crocodile, she strode out of the kitchen and through to the telephone.

Receiver up: "Morgan Orchards."

"Hello," Donald said.

"Oh."

"Have they arrived yet?"

Rendered forgetful by the welcome of his voice, Alma said, "Darling."

"The police," Donald asked. "Are they there?"

Remembering, Alma swung her head. She saw Warner watching. She said, "Yes, Mr. Smith. I'll be in touch. Good-bye." In putting the receiver down she realised that, good or bad, she was involved, the scheme was on.

The sergeant gave another professional throat-scrape. He said, "Who was that, Mrs. Morgan?"

"Customer."

"A customer?"

"Yes."

Behind Warner appeared the constable, who stayed long enough to whisper at close range. His superior changed wrists, changed back, said, "Looks as if someone was interrupted in doing a bit of digging, Mrs. Morgan. Fresh soil."

"Oh?"

"Was that you?"

"I told you I just got home, sergeant."

"Could be someone was digging a grave."

"I think not."

His eyes overacting, Warner asked, "Are you sure there's nothing you'd like to tell me?"

"Quite sure, thank you."

"All right. Let me put it to you this way. Have you done your husband an injury?"

"An injury?" Alma said. "No." She moved forward. "I'd like to have my tea now."

Also moving forward: "May I use your telephone, mum?"

"But of course, sergeant. Help yourself."

They bowed heads to each other in passing. Thinking it

all rather gorgeous in a strange way, Alma went to the kitchen. She poured her tea, which was perfectly mashed, which she appreciated as an omen, tea being so solid and British and traditional.

With a sensation of lurking power Alma sat at the table. Gratefully she sipped her tea, cup held in both hands, eyelashes trembling against the steam. Was Donald, she wondered, going to make a mess of it?

Refreshed, Alma was about to pour a second cup when Sergeant Warner came into view through the window. He gestured, drawing Alma up and across. She asked, "Well?"

"Your ceramic oven's on."

"I thought it would be."

His voice sounding high and plaintive through the glass, Warner asked, "What's in it, Mrs. Morgan?"

"What's in the kiln?"

"Yes."

"Private things."

"There's a clock on it and it looks to me as if it's been on for two hours. The oven, I mean."

"I knew what you meant, sergeant," Alma said, kind.

"Well look," Warner said, "if you were out all day, who switched it on?"

"Perhaps my husband."

"Who doesn't seem to be here anywhere."

"That's true."

"And you can't tell me where he is."

"No."

With faint sorrow Warner said, "Mrs. Morgan, I'll tell you straight I don't like this."

"Nor I."

"I think I ought to take a look inside that oven."

"That's up to you."

"Would you be kind enough to show me how to switch it off?"

Ten minutes later Alma and the policemen were standing by the kiln waiting for it to cool to a degree where a person could get near and look inside. The door was open. Through the space came waves of heat and a lessening in the stink of burnt stew which had been insulting the air.

Alma said, "I believe we might have some rain tonight."

"Not before time," the constable said.

Warner: "This's been the driest March for twenty years."

"That right, sarge?"

"Twenty years."

"Well now."

Her hand out, Alma said, "Seems a lot cooler."

Warner ordered, "Carry on, constable."

The young man stepped forward and aimed his flashlight through the doorspace, stooping to peer. "Bloody hell," he said slowly, following which he retreated, turned a glare on his superior and said, "There's bones and a sort of sludge. You best ring Exeter again."

Contrary to likeable conviction, pub guv'nors are delighted that the law obliges them to close afternoons from three until five-thirty. They need the break; they legitimately get shut of their tedious drunks; they earn fulsomely during the gulping, dribbling, bustling swill of the final half hour as customers battle to attain a mood that will allow them to greet the bell with a raucous laugh, not a pang of quiet terror.

Even more gratifyingly for your guv'nor, he is able to

get extra helpings of power's bliss by letting stay after time a favoured few, forelock-tuggers who themselves are gratified as, feeling special, they drink and whisper in the illicit gloom.

The unfavoured and unquenched, they go to the tween-time clubs, scruffies favoured by pimps, whores and a selection of society's other black sheep. These clubs come to life for a couple of hours every afternoon and several hours at night. You don't have to be sent by a version of Joe. Membership fee is one pound and drinks are above normal price, but there's nothing phony about the cellar's attar of colour, meaning sin and violence, and if people choose to whisper in the drab lighting it's because their flat-nosed neighbour at the bar might take exception to raised voices.

It was late afternoon when Molly went down steps to Neville's. The young soak of a doorman was asleep and sole remaining customers were playing cards, four men whose casual attitude told that they wished the stakes weren't so high.

In addition it told Molly, as she exchanged nods and calls with the four, that there was no knowledge to be kept hidden in respect of Henry Gosport. Molly knew the otherwise signs as well as any woman whose man was apt to go public with his philandering.

It had been the same at the three pubs and four clubs Molly had visited during the day, regular calls all. That no one had seen Henry she knew because she was asked about him everywhere: by way of being polite, showing interest, bestowing recognition, people always asked where a couple's non-present half was. Further, that no one had private information she knew from reading faces and voices.

Taking a stool at the bar Molly ordered a gin and pep-
permint. The yawning barman's question she answered
with the same story she had given to others.

"He's looking into a bit of business. Might be a while
before he shows his face again. You know."

"I know."

Sipping, acknowledging Neville's as her last try, Molly
accepted her story as probably true. The while might be a
night or a month, the bit of business was sure to be a
woman, since nobody knew anything that woman had to
be a mystery, and, as there was only one type of non-local
Henry would find intriguing, the mystery could only be
from another class or world.

But what would intrigue Henry, ran Molly's face-saver,
was the fact that the woman would herself be intrigued,
smitten, starry-eyed over gangster/jailbird/illiterate Henry
Gosport. So impressed by that would he be that his stay
with the socialite or executive or show-biz personality
would last until the glitter's light allowed him to see
clearly instead of dazzling. It had happened before.

Smiling, Molly got out a cigarette. As long as nobody
hereabouts knew, she could take it. Even, she was proud
in a way. He was quite a guy, that bastard of hers. She
certainly had no intentions of making a hole in the river.
Kill for Henry she would, yes, but herself she would never
kill, since that would be like killing Johnny too.

With a flourish, Molly struck a match and lit up. She
mused: I'm all right, me.

"They've arrived, the Exeter lot," Sergeant Warner said
as they rounded a bend on the village street.

A plain black van stood outside the police station, a

cottage differing from its neighbours only in the presence of an identifying sign, lit now against the dusk.

It was the first time anyone had spoken after they had driven away from the house, except for as they were passing a roadside cafe. Its recent enlargement brought admiring comments from Warner. The callousness, the indifference to what was taking place, had made Alma sink away from him on the car's back seat, appalled.

The constable stopped. He switched off and got out. As he went round to the other side Sergeant Warner said, quietly, "Remember, Mrs. Morgan, you don't have to say anything if you don't want to." He opened the door.

One minute later Alma was in a room that was elbow-rub packed with people. In addition to the full village force, there were three youngish men in plain clothes plus a jowly uniformed policewoman of fifty with a faint moustache. They created a hiss of busy talk, an atmosphere of subdued excitement. No one seemed especially interested in Alma, which she found annoying, but she preferred annoyance to being appalled.

Next she was in another room, more parlour than office, sitting low in an armchair. Far above her on straight chairs were two of the detectives. They wore the general post-war seediness as though proud not to be rich and smart, glad to be part of the Welfare State revolution, happy to look in need of a bath and a barber and frayless cuffs.

They had introduced themselves as Henderson and Bird, brusquely, as if it would have been better manners to leave names out of it. Henderson, who had grey teeth to top off a thin, unattractive face, asked a sudden:

"Where's the gun?"

"What gun?"

"Knew you'd say that. 'What gun?' I love it when they're awkward. Gives me the right to get awkward too."

Alma: "Shouldn't that policewoman be in here?"

The other detective said, "The gun you shot your husband with, Mrs. Morgan. Where is it?" He had a face to go with his manner—plump, comfy.

"No one said I shot my husband."

Henderson said, "I did. I said it. And I want to know what you did with the gun. The murder weapon."

Alma's right arm twitched. What an ugly word it was, she thought, murder. She said, "It seems to me you're taking a great deal for granted."

"Do you deny that your husband is dead? Do you deny that you put his body in the kiln? Do you deny that you were digging a hole to bury his skeleton?"

"I was in town all day."

The detective called Bird asked, "What's your boy friend's name, Mrs. Morgan?"

Alma coughed surprise. "My what?"

"Boy friend."

"What do you mean?"

"Perhaps you use the term lover. The man who you've been having an extra-marital relationship with. Would you tell me his name, please."

"I have no one like that. There's no such relationship. You've made a mistake."

"What if I told you we already know who he is."

"Then you could tell me and we'd both know."

"Snappy," the other man said. "Witty."

Alma: "Thank you."

Henderson went on, "Let's see how witty you can be about this. We have a witness who called in at the farm.

He heard the fight, heard the shots, saw you drag your husband out of the house and put him in the kiln."

"Valuable witness."

"I can bring him in to meet you, if you like."

"All right," Alma said pleasantly.

"Later."

The plump man said, "You'd save us all a lot of trouble, Mrs. Morgan, if you told us where we could find the gun. A Luger, isn't it?"

"I know nothing whatever about guns."

"We'll turn it up in the end, you know, so you might as well tell us."

"How long're you going to keep me here?"

"Did you put it up in an apple tree?"

"Am I under arrest?"

"Did you go away and toss it in a lake?"

Henderson said, "You are helping us with our enquiries, as the official terminology has it."

"I see."

"Why did you kill him?"

Folding her arms Alma said, "I'm getting tired of this." It was true.

"So're we. Myself, I'd rather be at home with the telly."

"I'd rather you were too, frankly."

He looked at his watch. "Do we have your permission to search your house?"

"You do not."

Bird: "Everything I say, Mrs. Morgan, makes you sound guilty. Surely that's not what you want."

"I want to go home."

"That depends on many things. One of them is you'll have to make a statement."

"About what?"

"Today. Your movements. You can dictate it while we go to have a look at the house and grounds."

"Without my permission?"

"We don't need it," the other detective said. "Nor a search warrant. There's ample evidence of a violent crime having been perpetrated."

Alma: "Then why did you ask?"

"To see what you'd say."

Within seconds the men had gone and Alma was sensing a change in the ambience, one as palpable as that brought by temperature, one, she had realised before the door opened again, caused by the detectives taking their joy away.

The jowly policewoman had pad and pencil. She sat on one of the chairs with a polite, dead, "I'll take down your statement, Mrs. Morgan, and then type it out. You can sign it after you've read it through."

"Very well. Thank you."

"Not at all."

It was two hours before the men came back. Meanwhile Alma had made her declaration, throughout same managing not to look at the woman's moustache; had been given sandwiches and a pot of tea; had stood and sat and paced; had begun to see that the greatest difficulty attached to the scheme, the greatest by far, was going to be boredom.

But Alma wasn't bored yet. Traveller in a strange land, she was afraid and stimulated. She had long since stopped hoping she was going to wake up to find it had all been one of those amazingly real dreams in which people who are ordinary to an outstanding degree do weird and terrible things.

With the men back in their seats, ambience brighter,

Bird wafted the sheets of paper he held. "I'll read your statement out to you, Mrs. Morgan."

Alma asked, "Did you put all the lights off before you left the house?" It was automatic.

Both policemen looked at her lingeringly, near admiringly, uncles with clever-cheeky niece. Henderson said, "There's an officer on guard."

"What for? Never mind. Is he trustworthy? Never mind."

Bird started to read aloud. Soon Alma said, "No, that's wrong. I'd forgotten when I was doing dictation. I didn't go in the car park. It was full. I parked in the street."

"So the attendant won't be able to vouch for you."

"Of course not."

Her next interruption was to say, "No, I didn't have an ice cream after all."

"Then the vendor can't say you were in town either."

"Quite."

The detective read on, finished, asked, "What about the sandwiches you had, if, as you state, you had lunch in Beal's?"

She explained about leaving the food in an alley, probably unseen by anyone. She agreed that it was also probable that no one in the restaurant would remember her. She told about throwing the cinema ticket away, as she always did.

"Piss-poor alibi," Henderson said.

Iron, Alma said, "I don't like your language."

"Where you're going, luv, you'll get used to it."

"I shall make an official complaint."

"You do. But for now, sign that statement."

"Not till it's been corrected."

The other detective said, "Let me tell you how we see

the case, Mrs. Morgan, starting from when you hit your husband with a vase, causing him to fall against the wall. You then ran up to the attic to get a gun. He followed to stop you. Being injured, he was too slow. When he got there you had the gun ready. You shot him several times."

Henderson: "Holding him under the armpits you dragged him downstairs. You put him in the kiln and set it going. You were starting to dig a pit to bury the bones in when the police arrived. We know all this so you might as well own up to it."

"Really?"

"Also tell us where the gun is."

"I have nothing more to say," Alma said. "I want to go home."

Henderson laughed. The other detective said, "Mrs. Morgan, perhaps we can strike a bargain."

"You'll let me go home if I tell you where the gun might be?"

"Afraid not. You'll have to stay here tonight. But we'll leave the questions until tomorrow if you help us find the gun. A bargain?"

"Yes, all right."

When the telephone rang, Bran was involved in the sexual act, making love with the stealth of a missionary who respects his wife so much she has a lot of headaches. Bran suspected the girl of being asleep. Although he knew you couldn't always tell with Anglo-Saxon women, he did realise that the lioness's share of a chicken and two bottles of wine on top of an evening's drinking was enough to put anyone away.

Therefore stealth. Awake the girl might go back to plugging the obscure pop group in which she formed one of the back-up singers, the group whose leader had neatly steered her onto Bran in the pub tonight when it came out that he was a reporter for a national daily.

Such connivance, an old game, Bran didn't mind, though he would have enjoyed the consequences more if he had been lying about his profession, shooting a line; but then he wouldn't have had the press credentials to show, thus provoking the leader into steering . . .

The telephone went on with its call signal.

Where another man, most men, would have found some way of ending the bedside clamour without doing so by actually answering, even when the girl might be asleep, Bran chose to be crass. He was not crass by nature. In certain aspects of his work, however, he had become cynical about permitting himself to be the rude, crude newshawk. No gentleman, he felt without stating, could ever make it to the top in tabloidism.

Easing up to a balance on one elbow, movement elsewhere on hold, Bran claimed the receiver. As expected at two o'clock in the morning, his caller was someone with the power to get away with destroying rest.

"Kelly here," a voice said.

"Never would've guessed."

"Wake up and ring me back in five minutes." The line died. This was standard procedure for night calls, editors having no time to waste on repeating themselves to semicomatose underlings who ought by ideal rights to be ticking with alertness.

Receiver back in its cradle, Bran hesitated. Should he or should he not finish what he had started with the girl? —he weighed. She wouldn't be hurt if he didn't, since she was almost certainly sleeping; if he did, the ultimate ruction would with equal near-certainty bring her conscious, where, group plugging apart, she could run interference in whatever it was Kelly had in mind, maybe that elusive big one.

Glad that hope still sprang eternal, Bran thought on in selfish vein, disregarding Ann or Anna. For one thing, hypnophilia was not all that great. For another, this assignment might include a romantic adventure, it wasn't unknown, and he would need to have his carnal wits and bits about him.

Like a coin dropping, that fast, Bran saw the absurdity of the situation. His body surged as it fought to contain a furious laugh. The girl murmured in appreciation.

Mouth open, lungs and belly locked, Bran got himself free of the embrace and out from under the covers, off the bed and over to an armchair, there to let go, face buried in a cushion. By the time his laughter had run its course, he had no need to think cold thoughts.

Nevertheless Bran had a pseudo-shower, a sponge-down standing in the tub along the hall. He would own a real shower-bath someday, he promised, when he was rich, when his big white ship came in.

Dressed (the call had to mean an immediate job), Bran called his editor. After naming people and places, Kelly said, "It's a murder. Wife shot husband and burned him to a cinder in a ceramic oven, of all things. That and the fact that they sound respectable could make it newsy."

"I agree."

"If you start driving now you'll be in on the ground floor. Any questions?"

"What if my car won't start?"

"Ring me straight back. I'll put someone else on it."

"It'll start. So long."

Minutes later, a note left for Ann or Anna, who could

even be Hannah, Bran was in his Austin disturbing Pimlico's quiet with engine revs and feeling an ache in the
muscles of his throat and stomach. It, he realised, had
been caused by laughter. He didn't laugh anywhere near
enough, that was the problem.

Although told by the constable when he brought
breakfast (milk, an orange, cheese on toast) that she
would be going to Exeter this morning, Alma was unpre-
pared for fast action.

No sooner was the meal over than the policewoman
came in with an important, "Off we go." Obeying, following into a corridor, Alma was still wondering what was
different about the woman today when she saw her start
to primp, brush at the uniform, fuss with her hair.

In the front room, packed as before, a man told Alma,
"Put this over your head." It was one of her raincoats
from home. She asked why. He said, "Press photogra-
phers."

Turning to the window Alma saw outside a crowd fifty
or sixty strong, mostly villagers, many of their faces familiar if not paired with names. Also there were three strang-
ers with large cameras.

She said, "I don't mind."

"We do," the man said. "Put it on."

Alma hooded herself with the coat, holding open a
front crack. She felt unpleasantly sleazy while also feeling
both securely masked and flatteringly mysterious.

Again Alma obeyed the policewoman's order to follow
her and in doing so realised what was different about the
jowly face: its moustache had gone.

Choir responds to baton's rise, talk swooped up instantly from a mumble as Alma went outdoors. During

the seconds it took for her to reach a van and get into its back, cameras flashed and voices said you never could tell, still waters ran deep, you would think butter wouldn't melt in her mouth, anyone could see she was hard as nails. The van doors closed with one of those shrill grinds that make the feet go strange.

Stamping, Alma pulled down a folding seat behind the cab, from which she was separated by glass and wire mesh. The latter came in useful to hold on to during the drive, since she was often in danger of being bounced off the seat.

Alma's straining to pick up information on her case from the bouts of conversation between uniformed driver and the policewoman resulted in frustration. They talked of diets, the Chief Constable's drinking, the new Humphrey Bogart film.

Outside a Gothic police station in Exeter the only people waiting were reporters, three of whom had been at the village. Constables came out to keep them all back as Alma, hooded, was led inside by the slow-moving policewoman.

The grim green room downstairs into which Alma was ushered alone had a table and four chairs, one ashtray, no windows. She sat with eyes closed until, after an hour, a man came in and leaned back on the wall with a superior smile.

He said, "So you're our little murderess, eh?"

Alma still hadn't responded when the door opened again. In came the two detectives from last night. Both stared at the stranger and Henderson asked, "What do *you* want?"

Shrugging, uneasy: "Not a thing. Having a look."

"Have a look somewhere else. This is our case. Hop it."

His smile a curdle, the man left. Bird asked, "Was he being a nuisance with questions, Mrs. Morgan?"

"No," Alma said. "He was going to tell me why the police don't want my photo in the papers."

"That's so people won't think they've seen you before, in person, relating to alibi, when all they've done is seen your photograph."

Henderson sat on the table. "But let's assume that your alibi is one hundred per cent true, luv, eh? In which case it could only have been prepared. And shrewdly. Nothing too definite. No having tea with the mayor. No asking a policeman the time. You even made little mistakes when talking about your day to make it seem natural."

Leaning far back so as not to hurt her neck in looking up at him, Alma asked, "Why would I do that?"

"Create an alibi? Why, to keep yourself clean while the boy friend was killing hubby."

"I have no boy friend."

"Everyone who telephones you, you call darling. Of course you do. You're the friendly type."

"That caller yesterday. I thought for a moment it was my husband."

"Forgetting he was dead?"

"You don't know he is."

"Come off it, luv," Henderson said happily. "But you can give us the number of the Mr. Smith you thought was your husband."

"I don't know him. He said his name was Smith."

"Darling Smith."

In trying to think up a telling remark to toss relating to Henderson's use of *luv,* Alma looked away. Her eyes came to Bird, who nodded as though accepting the move to himself of the interviewer rôle.

Taking a chair he said, "Mrs. Morgan, we have an open and shut case. It's pointless for you to go on stonewalling. Let me tell you what we've got. Okay?"

"If you must."

"So far, your alibi doesn't work. The blood in your house is the same type as Donald Morgan's—we got verification a few minutes ago from the armed forces. Photographs have been taken of the drag marks. We have the revolver and six shells—"

"Because of my guess that they'd be in that hole," Alma said.

"—and six melted bullets were found in the kiln. Our pathologist tells us the skeleton is that of a male, about thirty years old. Other matter in the kiln is human. Even at this early stage we have testimony from a neighbour that you and the deceased had several fights. And there'll be more stuff coming in. So why don't you tell us your side of the story, with all the extenuating circumstances."

Alma was grateful for the offer. In her hour alone here she had weighed pro with con and come to the conclusion that any time now she could reasonably get away with making a confession, seem to be accepting that she had lost. Sooner might have been seen as oddly defeatist. Later could make them wonder about the state of her mind—and if she were put away as insane the scheme would come to nothing.

However: in that respect Alma had also realised that were she to be convicted of homicide when the prosecution's brief was greatly aided by a confession, the pro-hanging lobby could say she would not have been convicted without it. She had therefore found a middle way.

"Very well," Alma said. "I think it is time I got around to the truth."

Bird said, "That's the spirit."

Henderson left the room.

Within minutes Alma was telling the policewoman, who took it down in shorthand, about that terrible argument with Donald over finances which had led to him throwing a vase at her, losing his balance and hitting his face on the wall before falling.

The detectives stood to listen, hovering, smoking, nodding Alma on. Their nods ended when she came to where Donald shouted he was sick of it, he was going to end it all.

Henderson: "End it?"

Alma: "Kill himself."

"Oh yes."

"He ran upstairs. I chased him. When I got to the attic he already had the revolver in his hand. I tried to get it away from him. We fought for it. He was too strong. He got it pointed at his chest and pulled the trigger."

Still ignoring the men, talking to the policewoman's shiny top lip, Alma said, "When I finally got over the shock and calmed down, I thought the situation over carefully. I saw there was a way of avoiding the awful stigma of suicide, and that was to destroy the remains. I would tell everyone that Donald had gone away, left me. I think it would've worked."

Drily, Henderson said, "May I remind you of a tiny detail? There were six bullets used, not one."

Alma told the lip, "I knew he was dead but I wanted to be sure before I put him in the kiln. I shot him five more times."

Bird said, "Go on."

Supposing the material found in with the skeleton to be meat or a boned animal that Donald had added (again bewailing the lack of planning, discussion), Alma said, "I dug a hole for the shells and gun, got them partially hidden and then quickly set off to create some kind of alibi. It had just occurred to me that, if things went wrong, I might be suspected of having killed my husband."

Henderson gave a mild groan, the largest of its several ingredients being derision, which afforded Alma a satisfaction which puzzled her until she realised she was aware of a danger: what if her innocence was believed?

She glanced up, saw no belief in either face, continued, "I drove to Exeter, walked about a bit, went into the pictures and out again by an emergency exit and drove back home." On this she congratulated herself, knowing all could be spoiled if people, people she hadn't noticed, were to come forward and swear they had seen her in town. She ended, "Then the village police rolled up. That's all."

Henderson said, "Neat story."

The other detective said with no attempt at drama, "Mrs. Donald Morgan, you are now under arrest on suspicion of having unlawfully killed your husband Donald Frederick Morgan and it is my duty to warn you that anything you say now or later may be taken down in writing and used in evidence against you."

Calm, Alma said she wanted to apply for Legal Aid. The policewoman asked her if she would like a nice cup of tea.

Donald, waiting outside a suburban newspaper shop, was not in the best of moods. The weather, yes, was fine; his complete removal from the area of home, yes, had been accomplished before daylight, and, by getting a lift, he had arrived in Plymouth. All well and good. But he had needed to erode his limited funds by buying items he should have thought to pack in the knapsack—a comb, soap, a razor, toothpaste.

What made it worse for Donald was his being unable to accept through several tries that in the razor's case his forgetfulness had been unconsciously intentional, that, naturally, he had planned on growing a beard. Failure was due to his knowing how suspicious an unshaven man would look, more tramp than hiker, a magnet for police attention.

Into the kerb steered a van, slowing. After a bundle had been thrown out of its back, the van shot on. A boy came out of the shop to collect the early edition of the Plymouth evening newspaper. Before long Donald was reading a copy.

On page two, under a photograph of a raincoat and part of a policewoman, was the headline HOUSEWIFE HELPS WITH MURDER INVESTIGATION. The story was roughly what Donald had expected, save in one glaring respect.

Although Alma Morgan was mentioned several times, the man she had allegedly killed earned only one mention, at the end, when it was brought out that he had been a witness in a murder trial some fifteen months before.

The newspaper got crumpled as Donald pushed it into his knapsack, telling himself he supposed it would come in handy for something or another.

Next, walking on, Donald's self-telling was that what he had planned to grow was, of course, a moustache, yet had absent-mindedly like the proverbial professor forgotten that he would need to shave the rest of his jaw. Of course.

Molly got a shock on hearing the shout, "Dad's in the paper again!" She stopped walking so forcefully she nearly dropped her bag of shopping. It again nearly fell when she made a grab for Johnny as he went scooting by from behind on one rollerskate, followed by other boys, courtiers dog prince. They all went out of sight.

Turning, Molly headed back for the shops. During this short walk she got from three separate people the tossed report that Henry was in the press, though they weren't so much passing on information as making comment on what they obviously assumed she already knew. In order not to disabuse them as well as be thought wanting, she smiled, as they themselves were smiling.

Which, the good cheer, took the panic out of Molly's shock. It was penury help. Sneezer freed of his spasms by a fright, she felt a loss without feeling a gain.

In the shop Molly bought all three of London's evening newspapers. Outside, shopping held between her feet, she began to scan. Finding nothing, she started on the next paper and was held by a name she had already seen in paper one without getting caught by.

She read about people she had met, Donald and Alma Morgan, so astonished at the man having been murdered, and possibly by his wife, that she forgot Henry until coming upon his name, which made her head jerk.

So that was fine, Molly thought in folding the newspaper. Henry wasn't in trouble. The reverse, in a way. The arse who had given false evidence against him was dead, done in by his wife. Wherever Henry was, he'd be having a good laugh.

Molly laughed herself as she remembered the way she had been treated by Donald Morgan, who had bustled her out of the house like something cheap and nasty. There was some justice in the world after all, Molly allowed.

After thousands of years of civilisation, lair is still so vital that the place a person most craves to be when in danger, sick or abused, is bed. Not any bed. His own bed.

Alma, risking a criminal offence, unwell with worry, slapped across her sense of propriety, had spent last night in a fair imitation of home insofar as it was in a real bedroom. You can't put a respectable woman in one of them bloody dungeons, the sergeant's wife had said. There had thus been the minimum of additional trauma.

Today Alma was spending most of her time lying on a bunk in a cell, being she had nothing to sit on apart from the open commode, bunk impractical for sitting because of the low bunk above, which was similarly penalised by the ceiling. She was drab in spirit. Twice she had been close to tears; once because the lunch tray was set out so pretty, once at the distant sound of a dog barking.

Repeatedly Alma had told herself that this, the beginning, was going to be the hardest, that when she had got through the first day or two the rest would be a cakewalk. If others could endure privation for an ideal, so could she. When you considered what martyrs some women had been, such as Suffragettes on hunger strike being force-fed with tubes down their throats like paté geese, Christians torn apart by lions . . .

Alma had succeeded in making herself totally wretched. She now responded with a snap when the door opened to admit a young policewoman who said a colourless, "Your legal representative's here, Morgan. Come on." Alma followed.

She had already met John Randolph Whitehall once, earlier, within an hour of having chosen from a list the name she most liked the tang of. She had not been disappointed.

Whitehall was a gallant of sixty who resembled an ancient, sly convict. Small and wiry, wearing morning dress, where he should have had the senior advocate's long white hair he had a speckle of silver bristles; in place of the expected noble features he had a cherry nose, sharp eyes and a mouth which seemed to be saying it was better to express contempt than defeat.

Yet John Randolph Whitehall impressed Alma as being perfect. He appeared clever enough to put up a good, believable fight but not shrewd enough to win. Besides, she liked him.

Their meeting earlier had been precisely that, a meeting, a heeding of words, a mutual scrutiny of face and mien. Acceptance over, the barrister had gone off to study the prosecution's view of the case.

In the interview room, policewoman closing herself out, John Randolph Whitehall used his eloquent arms to usher Alma into a chair, bowed as though to compliment her on her cool style, sat himself.

He patted the table. "Well now."

Alma said, "At least they let us talk alone."

"You haven't been convicted of anything yet, Mrs. Morgan." The voice was low, inviting confidences. "Technically you're among the innocent."

"I should hope so."

"You'll be treated fairly well and your meals will be brought in from a cafe."

"What happens next, please?"

Whitehall said, "Tomorrow or the next day, we go into court. There it will be decided if the Crown's case is strong enough. If it is, and there seems no doubt about that, you will be ordered to stand trial—for the capital crime of murder."

"In London?"

"No, here in Exeter. The May Assizes. In about two months."

"Meanwhile what?" Alma asked. "I don't suppose there's any hope of bail."

"No. Most likely they'll move you to Exeter Gaol."

"My treatment will continue nice?"

"Perhaps a little more casual."

"I'll still be innocent."

Whitehall leaned forearms on his briefcase to ask, "And are you innocent, Mrs. Morgan?" He was smiling, lightly, father asks daughter if she likes his new tie.

Alma looked down. She was tempted to tell the truth, which annoyed her, this instability, but she nevertheless began thinking on a different tack.

The lawyer said, "Police don't go into court saying to the judge and jury, in effect, here is the evidence, the rest is up to you, we don't know if this person is guilty or innocent. They say, This person is guilty. And, of course, more often than not, guilty he is. Police don't take many chances on losing."

Alma looked up. "I understand."

"So how about you, Mrs. Morgan?"

"Have you read my statement? The second one? Well, what do you think, from that?"

"That events could be exactly as you stated," Whitehall said. "Let's look at it, mm?" From his briefcase he brought papers. His sorting over, he read the pseudo-con-fession aloud, glancing at Alma as commas, looking at her pointedly for full stops. Finished, he asked, "How does it sound to you, Mrs. Morgan?"

"Not bad."

"Is it true?"

"What if I said no? What if I said I was guilty? Would you still take the case?"

"Say it and we'll find out."

Alma said, "The statement's more or less true." She had decided that John Randolph Whitehall would be a sticker, that if he thought his client was innocent he would go to fantastic lengths, be a mover of stars and mountains, in order to get her off, which must not happen.

She said, "The truth, Mr. Whitehall, is that at that moment I believe I changed sides, the moment when we were struggling for the gun. I wanted Donald dead."

The barrister looked at her steadily. "Yes?"

"I was trying to make the gun fire, and I think Donald was trying to keep it from doing so. He'd also changed his mind." She nodded. "Yes, I wanted my husband dead."

"Perhaps he was trying to kill you."

"No, not Donald. He couldn't kill anything. That's why we went in for apples instead of rabbits or chickens."

Whitehall said, "Mrs. Morgan, in a heated, panicky moment like that one in the attic nobody can say as an absolute what thoughts are paramount. It would be better if you forgot what you just said."

"What about when I'm on the witness stand?"

"You won't be a witness, you'll be the prisoner at the bar. I won't be putting you on for questioning, I believe."

"We have the choice?"

When Whitehall had finished explaining the process he picked up more papers. "Let's hear this one." He read out Alma's first declaration, using the same optic punctuation as before. Papers lowered, he asked, "How does that sound?"

"Awkward."

"Yes, and far more true than the other."

"But the police will have checked it out before charging me with the crime."

With features kind: "My dear young lady, the police don't attempt to prove an alibi true, they only attempt to break it if it interferes with their case."

Alma said, "That doesn't seem terribly just."

Kindness enduring: "The police are not particularly in-terested in justice, Mrs. Morgan. That's for idealists, dreamers, romantics. A policeman is basically an ordinary chap, one whose career depends on his record—arrests and convictions. He has a family to support, children to educate, a mortgage to pay off. Advancement is of great consequence to him."

"Now that sounds definitely dishonest."

Putting the papers away, John Randolph Whitehall said, "If your average man on the police force is less hon-est than your average man in the street—and he is—he can hardly be blamed for it."

"Come now."

"Man in the street might go all his life without having his honesty tested, strained, but with an officer it's a regu-lar feature of his work. Even though he starts out straight, as most do, he eventually steps into the first hole, accepts a fiver to look the other way—when, that is, an arrest is valueless to him in his career. From there it gets deeper and more labyrinthine."

"I'm shocked," Alma said, not in her rôle, putting a protective hand on her chest. "You speak so easily of brib-ery and corruption."

"It's a fact of my professional life, Mrs. Morgan. And please remember, it's all a matter of viewpoint. If, say, an officer plants evidence on a suspect, he is not being corrupt as he sees it. He believes the man to be guilty, *knows* him to be guilty, of a past crime if not the present one, and sees no reason why he shouldn't go to prison. He believes he is doing society a favour."

Patting herself: "But it's still totally dishonest, isn't it, Mr. Whitehall?"

The lawyer put on his light smile. "And how about you, Mrs. Morgan. Are you being honest totally?"

"As close as I can be," Alma said, which, she told herself smugly, was true.

"And you're not shocked at being incompletely so? At admitting it so easily?"

Unsmug, uncomfortable: "Whose side are you on?"

"Our side, young lady," Whitehall said, gentle. "We want to win our case, as the innocent should always win. And we are innocent, aren't we?"

"That's another matter of viewpoint. I told you my desires in the struggle. It's quite possible I was responsible for turning the revolver in the right direction and for forcing Donald to pull the trigger."

Nodding, John Randolph Whitehall said, "It's also quite possible that you weren't even there."

"What?"

"That you spent your day in town exactly as you stated. That you knew nothing of what had happened at the house until you got back. That, worthily but misguidedly, you are protecting the real murderer."

"Who?"

"Your lover."

"Sorry," Alma said, meaning it and to help in showing

this shaking her head sincerely. "Donald and I are the only people involved. Sorry."

Slugs on a clean window, the twelve men leaned against the wall of sanitation green in every state but proper, in every pose but neat. It was as though they were trying to outdo each other in disdain for style, or afraid of being thought anything other than urbane, cynical, untouchable on the emotions.

Most extreme was a man who had sunk to a squat and wore his trilby tipped over his eyes. Least so was a man whose hangover matched, being as mild as his lean.

He had done fairly well altogether over the past couple of days, Bran reminded himself. True, he hadn't been the first to find out that the victim had given evidence at the trial of Henry Gosport, to his embarrassment, since he was the only reporter here to have covered that trial and to have actually met Donald Morgan. True also, he was one of the last to learn that Alma Morgan had been formally charged, but that was hardly a scoop.

The next leaner passed an upturned hat. Accepting it, Bran dipped in, scuffled among the pieces of folded paper, took one out, passed the hat on to his neighbour.

On the other hand, Bran continued heavily in his determination to finish this rub with soothing oil, the pictures he had sent to Kelly were tops—the accused peering out from inside a coat, angles on the Morgan house, close-ups of the kiln and an artistic panorama of apple trees. Also there had been interviews with two locals and Sergeant Warner. Furthermore, other papers were beginning to ease out the first name, the Kiln Killing, and use the one he himself had originated: the Orchard Murder.

Bran was still ruffling himself about that, thrush in the

sun, when his neighbour asked while passing the hat back down the line, "What number you get?"

Paper unfolded: "Seven."

"I'm twelve."

"A good 'un."

The man said, "Want to swap?"

"I don't care. Okay."

Exchange made, Bran set to musing on future plans in connexion with this case. They included another try at finding the man who had telephoned the police anonymously after having heard violent goings on at Morgan Orchards, doing a piece on his meeting with victim Donald Morgan outside the Old Bailey, and perhaps an interview with Henry Gosport to get his opinion on Morgan's sticky end.

Regarding the immediate future, Bran thought cozily, when business was over here he would have a luxury lunch after a drink or several, enjoy being on an expense account while the enjoying was good, out in the field.

A nearby door opened.

With the alacrity of boys heading for algebra, the reporters assembled themselves and began to move. This was a duty attendance. Nothing newsworthy was likely to happen, but you had to be on hand just in case.

They filed into court.

On benches in the press section Bran sat among his colleagues, not one of whom had made cushions out of folded coats or assaults on the best positions.

As every newsman knew, they wouldn't be here long. The lottery, whose winner would be given ten shillings by each of the other eleven men, was on how long the proceedings would last, five minutes to fifteen. Outcome was not in doubt.

The accused was brought in.

Kempt as the moral ideal of the social class she belonged to, Alma Morgan was the unlikeliest candidate for the prisoner's box in a murder trial you were liable to find, Bran reckoned as he scrutinised the woman with the care of a blind-dater.

He still went on staring after the gavel had hit the hearing open. He was taken to an unusual degree by Alma Morgan's manner, her stance, which gave the impression that she thought she had done something clever, like a nurse who gets the better of her decrepit patient.

Bran wondered what was going on in her head. Her way of attending acutely to what was being said reminded more of a fascinated spectator than the endangered. Cat cornered by a mouse, she seemed fearless.

Sensing the growth of tension round him, Bran looked at his watch. Six minutes had gone from the gavel. One man made a sound of disgust. Bran, himself now tense on account of that five pounds ten, did what the other reporters were doing, shared his attention between watch and speakers.

Seven minutes passed and then, at close to eight, the gavel ended it, accused having been ordered to stand trial for murder at the Assizes. Rising, patting himself to find ten shillings, Bran was thinking of a way to wangle the money on his expense account.

FOUR

During the following weeks Molly never realised how she had changed in that respect and would have been insulted if anyone had been able to point it out to her. A real mouthful, that's what the omnipotent anyone would have received in return had he said she no longer tensed at the sound of a car out in the street; listened to footfalls; visited out-of-the-way pubs and clubs; scanned about constantly when shopping; looked for signs in people's faces; made discreet enquiries while out of her own manor; had he said, in sum, that she was no longer expecting the imminent appearance of the man in her life.

Molly did realise, yes, that sometimes she gave a thought to the Orchard Murder. But the thoughts were in a half-submerged fashion.

Molly had no wish to step right out in front of herself like a twin sister, turn, fold her arms confidentially and ask the question, Did Henry kill Donald Morgan?

To Molly, not only was the possibility daft and far-fetched, not only radio-serial melodramatic, it suggested the gravest danger for a man who couldn't reasonably expect to beat another murder charge. It suggested, in fact, the rope.

That matter could be solved, of course, as Molly knew, by the victim's wife being found guilty. However, as Molly further knew, if that happened it could eventually prey on her mind, especially if the woman was executed, and might even tend to come between Henry and herself.

So Henry being the one who had killed Donald Morgan was best not thought about on the surface, Molly had hiddenly decided. Best in spite of the way he had looked when she had told him of her visit to Morgan Orchards over the Appeal. Best in spite of those "proofs" which had been peripherally acknowledged: his several odd remarks about people who should be made to pay for bearing false witness, his having the money and connexions to buy a gun, his being the kind who never forgot a grudge, his departure from home neatly fitting with times of trains to that area, his complacent attitude to killing.

Molly kept her twin sister unbirthed. She knew very well that the man she loved was foolishly, passingly under the spell of some whorish rich bitch, not hiding out because he had done someone in.

Donald stayed around Plymouth. He camped sometimes in fields (with or without the farmer's permission), sometimes on official tenting sites. During rains of consequence, which came in faithful April, he stayed in those youth hostels where everyone is welcome who looks like an amateur wanderer, the professionals being barred.

In one such place Donald got on close terms with a Danish girl. One of a quartet cycling around Britain, she agreed to a walk, a drink and a chat in his room. She stayed the night. She said she never could resist a man with a moustache. Next morning she cycled off with many a fond glance back.

While pretending to be unsure if his after-pleasure came from the hearty sex or the flattery of having been desired, and by a girl ten years his junior at that, Donald suspected himself of owning a glow of pride at his caddish lack of remorse over the adultery, all of which kept obscure the probability that he had straightforwardly enjoyed putting Alma down.

Two days later, camping alone again, Donald counted his money. It was low. Better not wait till he was broke altogether, he reckoned cheerfully as he sorted through the packet of stamps he had brought along. He chose a 1910 five-centimo, which he took with him when, in fresh khakis, he set out for the centre of the city.

The stamp and coin shop Donald first found was a cramped affair in a measly street. He searched on until coming across a more prosperous-looking business on a main thoroughfare. The owner, a small older woman with darty movements, listened impassive as the Frenchman on a walking tour explained in poor English with a fierce accent about this, his way of circumventing currency regulations, the law against taking cash out of the country.

The woman put a cupped hand six inches from her ear, demonstrating. "Could you say that last bit again, please."

Repeating, Donald assured himself there would be no problem in this regard. Everybody in Britain had become familiar with and complacent about short-cuts and fiddles, understandings and eye-closings.

Hand down, the woman spoke again. This time the language she used wasn't English, it was one Donald recognised as French, though that was the extent of his recognition. He went hot. He smiled foolishly.

The woman said, *"Comment?"*

Donald licked his smiling lips. Abruptly he said, "Pliz. I need to practice ze English."

"Yes. Excuse me. I will give you the catalogue price for your stamp. All right?"

"Zat will be correct."

Transaction over, Donald left the shop without his heat but feeling a vague disappointment. He quickly cheered up on recalling how brilliantly he had wriggled out of that tricky corner.

On the whole Donald was relishing his strange adventure, though he preferred to think not in terms of relish but hardy resistance to despondency. He liked sleeping in a tent, cooking simple meals, sitting dreamily by a fire at night. Urbanly, he liked to stroll, stand to watch the passing scene, ask directions of policemen.

Tired of solitude, he could find company on the official sites, where, being older than your average camper, he earned deference, gave advice, and was able to hint at the existence of another, more exciting and romantic story behind jovial hiker Jim Wilson. He cultivated a mysterious smile.

Donald's favourite fire-gazing dwell was on his triple triumph. Not only had he escaped death at the hands of a vicious killer, he had turned the event from a minus to a plus. Not only had he changed his life, he had been given a magnificent cause. Not only had society been ridded of a dangerous criminal, it was going to be ridded of a barbaric practice.

Particularly Donald liked reflecting on his life being changed. It was 100 per cent true, he knew. Things would never be the same again. No celebrity could get away with living like ordinary people. When you joined the ranks of the immortals you had to take on different standards and attitudes—though there was no reason why you couldn't retain the common touch, for use on specific occasions.

In respect of his scheme, the one he had created and set in vibrant motion, Donald felt confident if somehow a shade uncomfortable. This last he supposed was due to his wife, to her doing some of the hardship-bearing without him by her side to give support. Although he stressed for himself his inability to change matters, he failed to shake off the discomfort, which in sighed resignation he blamed on his sensitivity.

That the case had disappeared from the newspapers was pleasing to Donald. His wife now had freedom from the glare of publicity. When he did at length come across a squib, in the Exeter paper he read regularly in public libraries, it was merely a mention about the large number of letters Mrs. Morgan was receiving. The majority were abusive. Some of the reverse were proposals of friendship or marriage.

"She happens to have a husband already," Donald said aloud. Tough, he stared back at the two old men who were also in the reading room and who had turned on him looks of surprise and hope.

The next time Donald spoke aloud to himself was after breakfast one morning, lying on his sleeping bag to wait out a shower. He said, "Why don't I go and visit her, in disguise?"

The idea took his breath away. He had to sit up to pant. Eased, he considered, flinging pro after con after pro on the scales, making most weight with the granite fact that his disguise need not be all that effective, since it was unlikely he would meet at Exeter Gaol anyone who would recognise him.

What ended it, what sent Donald slowly horizontal

again, was his realising that he would be asked for identification. He listened to the rain.

However, his morning he saved by recalling those letters. If he couldn't visit his wife in person during her tiresome time he could certainly write her a letter, give assurance of his total support and love.

A pleasant hour Donald spent over composition. Enigmatic, that was his style. Even so, through the use of intimate reference he made the sender's identity wealthily clear, denying that scrawled *An Unknown Admirer* at the bottom.

Donald felt worthy. In a nearby town he asked a constable the way to the postbox he could see in the distance.

After the hearing, Bran's personal interest in Alma Morgan, because of her mien, that elusive essence, lasted for three and a half days, until the Tower Bridge Bombing hit the headlines. Twenty sleepless hours he spent chasing policemen and rivals all over the city.

That done, suicided bomber without news value, being simply insane, Bran thought again about the Orchard Murder, but now from a professional standpoint.

What he ought to do was follow through on those ideas, he urged. He should write pieces on Donald Morgan and Henry Gosport, as well as have a go at tracing the anonymous caller. At the same time, in that part of the world, why not interview the victim's mother, who had moved into the orchard house.

What did she think every day at least once when her eye fell on the kiln, where her son was reduced to nothing?—Bran wondered as he made his way upstairs in the *Daily Standard* building. Must be as hard as nails.

He went into Kelly's office. The crime editor was bald,

swarmy fat, a mess of dribbled cigarette ash. Though he rarely put one to his lips, and more rarely still inhaled smoke, he was never without a cigarette in his swollen hands.

"Not bad," Kelly said, brisk as a cutter-dead.

Sloping over the desk Bran said, "Two or three days should do the trick."

"I can see that."

"All I need is a chit for expenses."

His manner honed, Kelly said, "Be a waste of effort, Peel, come to think of it. If the coppers can't find an anonymous caller, neither can you."

"You don't know me. Once I get on a trail, I don't give up. I'm a bloodhound."

"Forget it. Go away. I'm busy."

"The mother," Bran said. "She's living in the house where it all happened. How's that for ye human interest crap?" He was being facetious to hide his earnestness, which attitude could turn any old Fleet Streeter irreversibly sour.

"Who gives a stuff?" Kelly said.

"Newspaper readers?"

"Go away."

A week later the *News of the World* came out with a middle spread, an as-told-to by Mrs. James Morgan: "I Always Knew My Son Would Be Murdered Someday."

Bran would have gone to El Vino to get drunk except for knowing that every single reporter who ever overworked his drinking arm out of sorrow had the same excuse to sloppily repeat—editorial blindness. Bran had no need to remind himself that he was, after all, unique.

Making sure an open copy of the *News of the World* was left on Kelly's desk, Bran used his own time to knock out

"Born To Be A Murder Victim." It was an interview with Donald Morgan conducted in the street outside the Old Bailey during the Gosport trial. The interview was 97 per cent imagination. Bran, however, was morally without a qualm, having somewhere recently accepted that, as a tabloid reporter, his job was not to inform but entertain. Where once he might have considered the piece a punch in truth's belly, he saw it now as a duty well performed. He sent it up to Kelly.

On the drive to Stepney, Bran whistled. He also played with titles. "Fate Has Her Revenge" was one he tried for the piece he would do on Henry Gosport. Another was "Murder Rebound: How A Witness Who Gave Evidence Against An Alleged Murderer Was Himself Murdered."

Bran turned the car into Can Lane, drew to a stop in front of number 10. Alighting in saunter style he tipped his hat to one side as he went to the house. He knocked. The first answer was a twitch in the curtains of the nearby window, the second a foot of space growing between door and jamb.

"Yeah?"

Shifting his gaze down to the source, Bran saw the face of a boy. He said, "Hello, sonny."

"What you want?" the boy asked, a welcome for famine.

"I've got something for Mr. Gosport."

"What is it?"

"Well, it's a message."

"Send a postcard."

Smiling patiently when he wanted to grab the stunted wretch and shake him hard, Bran said, "I'd like to see Mr. Gosport to give him this message in person."

The boy said, "We're sick to death of being bothered by you bloody reporters."

"*Is* Mr. Gosport at home?"

"He's in New York."

"All right. Is Miss Harker in?"

"She's gone to Paris for a month or two."

"What's your name, sonny?"

"Danny Kaye," the boy said. "Ta-ra." The door closed.

Driving away flat, Bran supposed he had best shelve the idea for a piece on Henry Gosport, who could well be inside the house, as could his consort. If the gangster didn't okay the project beforehand, and didn't like what he read afterhand, he could get nasty. Bran, as Bran was ready to admit, had no sully of courage to steer him wrong.

Later, telephoning Kelly about the Morgan interview, he heard, "Not bad, Peel. But too late. That Orchard thing's dead. Maybe when the trial starts I can use this. We'll see."

Bouncing back as usual, Bran shrugged the disappointments light. They were forgotten next day, when he became involved in the Northwood Kidnapping. He was excited. This, he knew, could be the big one.

The food in Exeter Gaol was awful. Yet even that, the single mark of genuine black, Alma had been able to bleach. Here was her opportunity to get rid of the few pounds she had been talking about losing for years, five at least. From a hearty eater she turned into a nibbler, picky.

As to quarters, Alma had a four-bunk cell to herself, which enabled her to constantly change beds. The cell was a luxury not granted to the already convicted, she was assured, those prisoners from whom she was isolated.

Lightly, Alma told her assurers, "I could do with less luxury and more company."

They were not amused. Nor were they offended. The wardresses seemed determined to demonstrate that they were void of emotions.

Alma's solitary state was not oppressive, and sometimes a female detainee was put in with her for hours or a whole day, a real treat, one she would relive afterwards, the stories and whispered confidences.

A remand prisoner with certain privileges, Alma had all the reading matter she could manage, morning and afternoon exercise in a courtyard (alone, but there was a cat), radio via earphones of an evening. She was treated well. Her request to be allowed to clean out the cell every day had been granted. There were scores of letters to answer, and she loved writing letters.

Alma's only visitor at first was John Randolph Whitehall, her mother-in-law staying condemningly away and there being no one else close enough to her to apply for a visitor's card. To one of the temporary cellmates Alma confessed her regret at needing to be hard, to deny access to the dozens of friends who were begging to come.

For John Randolph Whitehall's sake on his visits Alma acted initially subdued, near beaten. This she eased off before he left in order to show him what a tonic he was. She had no artifice, however, when on almost every visit she told the lawyer how sorry she was at being unable to help, admit to shielding a third person—brother, dear friend, lover.

One day Whitehall said, "Tomorrow, Mrs. Morgan, you'll be seeing a psychiatrist."

Uneasy: "I will?"

"The first in a series of sessions."

"You arranged it?"

"No no. I abandoned that angle long ago. The Crown are doing this. They want their case watertight. It would be damaged if doubts were cast on your sanity."

In the beginning Alma looked upon the daily sessions with Dr. Hazlett with favour. It was an hour of company, the interview room was a nice change of scene, the psychiatrist, big untidy bear of a man, had a friendly way with him and a sharp sense of humour. They had many a laugh over Alma's responses to tests, questions and ink-blots.

Following the third session Alma came to the icy understanding that Hazlett could mistakenly conclude that she was unfit to plead, being of unsound mind; could, further, state the same in court not from perceived evidence but, having grown to like her, as an act of kindness, camaraderie.

Thereafter Alma went to the sessions warily. Her answers to questions she chose with care in an effort to seem sane while treating the doctor coolly.

Although unhappy about the latter, Hazlett being such a charmer, and worried that he might consider the changed attitude peculiar, Alma could think of no other way to handle the situation. There were times when she felt desperate for advice.

Nonetheless she reckoned to have succeeded with the alienist. On his penultimate visit he asked, "You haven't taken a dislike to me, have you, Mrs. Morgan?"

"Not in the least, doctor."

"But you're different."

Alma said, "Well, I couldn't go on fighting despair for ever."

A letter came from Donald. Alma had realised who the anonymous author was after reading only three sentences.

The first contained a play on one of his pet names for his wife, second used an expression which had become a family joke, third misspelled the word she herself always got wrong.

Worriedly Alma read on. From the repetition of *nod* (Don in reverse) to the giving of his birthdate in an astrology mention, the letter formed a potent statement to the continuing existence of Donald Frederick Morgan.

Although she didn't destroy it, knowing no one else was going to be a reader and that, as a factor in the scheme, it ought to be preserved, Alma was unsettled by the letter. Against one beneficial emotion—pleasure at proof of Donald's devotion—there were three to give discomfort: embarrassment at her husband's schoolboy wit, annoyance that he thought her so dense she would need extensive hinting before guessing authorship, a nudge for the slumbering worry that Donald could do something foolish and thus throw the whole scheme away.

Molly found herself tense on the day the trial of Alma Morgan was due to start down in Exeter. If the town had been within reasonable driving distance she might have rented a car and attended, she told herself at breakfast, which was a lying way of asking, Shall I go?

Briefly, that little thrill of indecision, the excitement of being lost, sent a current of tingles up Molly's thighs from knee to groin.

Her legs shot up straight. They bumped the table, rattling dishes and slopping milk and bringing Johnny erect from listening to his Rice Krispies.

He asked, "What's up?"

Molly rapped, "Close it."

"Eh?"

She came on sweet with, "Nothing, luv. I was thinking about something." The false grin she hitched on stayed there until her son gave his interest back to the cereal.

Of course she wasn't going anywhere, Molly fumed, happy to so fume, be distracted. As if she didn't have enough to do without driving off to the ends of the earth so she could gloat over the death of a man who had tried to swear Henry's life away and had as good as thrown her out of his house. Christ.

Although this and its similars ended the question of trial attendance, there was no end for Molly's tension. It, she later told herself with complete acceptance despite knowing it to be untrue, was due to her pre-menstrual state. She even chewed two of her calcium tablets; and afterwards did gain a breath of satisfaction from cursing their incompetence.

By having a walk, by buying a light bulb that she didn't need and left in the shop anyway, and by calling on neighbours without having the slightest understanding or recollection of what was said, Molly brushed the long morning under the rug of her mind.

When her son came home for lunch from school she was bile and syrup again. She made him wash his hands twice and clean his plate, she told him he was the best boy in the land and promised to take him to see the Derby.

Early afternoon Molly ached along with sighs and chores, meanwhile declining to recognise what she was sighing about, refusing to see the chores as useless.

She went to the shops in good time for the arrival of the first edition of the evening newspapers. Casually she bought the only one to be available as yet, its front page hectic about the Northwood Kidnapping, back to life on account of the hostage had been released. The Orchard Murder trial was on page three.

Molly had to smile, it was so silly of her to look first at the report's byline, a thing she couldn't remember ever having done before. Somehow she had expected, she knew, to see there that reporter's name, the man she had met and fancied, the man she had watched from behind the curtains a few weeks ago, wary of going to the door as she didn't trust herself; expected the name in spite of knowing he worked for a different paper altogether, a national daily.

Her tension gone, Molly stood in the shop to read about the trial's morning. It had been spent in establishing identity of victim and outlining a biography of prisoner.

A statement made by Alma Morgan and read by the prosecution showed she agreed that her late husband had broken the same two bones which the skeleton owned evidence of having fractured; an expert said the skeleton came from a recently alive male, an Anglo-Saxon, height and build somewhat above average, aged between thirty and forty; a man from the police laboratory and another from Army Records made clear that smears of blood on the Morgan property were the same blood-type as that belonging to Donald Morgan.

Counsel for the Crown, Peter Wembley, QC, asked the court what more proof could anyone want. Counsel for the defence, John Randolph Whitehall, said none, no one was disputing identity, it was time his learned friend moved along with the prosecution's flaccid case.

The prisoner at the bar, her biography told, had been found in an alley by a beggar, an old man seeking food. Approximately five hours old, she was wrapped in newsprint. The old man took her to a nearby cafe, whose chef-owner drove her to a hospital. Over the following months and years the foundling passed through several agencies, before being settled in the Dr. Barnster Home for Christian Waifs. She stayed there until age fourteen. Along with two other orphans she was put into boarding school, choice of candidates made by IQ test, fees paid by an ex-Barnster girl who had acquired wealth. At eighteen Alma Cook became independent, sharing a flat with a friend, taking work as a secretary in an engineering firm. At twenty-four she met Donald Morgan. They married a year later.

The impression taken in by Molly, a receptive, was that only a baby of poor quality would be abandoned by its mother, that orphans tended to be callous, that people who beat others at tests were shady, that those with wealthy patrons were toadies, that secretaries were glorified prostitutes, and that any girl who stayed single until in her mid-twenties obviously had something wrong with her.

Molly found the report a consolation. In a better balance of mind she went home and made Johnny a special tea. Later, leaving him with the television, she went to see a client as part of passing time until the final editions of the newspapers came out with accounts of the afternoon's legal doing.

With a hundred Welsh blankets to get rid of, the client was eager to please. He fed Molly champagne cocktails on top of flattery. She was mellow with alcohol and fondness for herself when, in a treat taxi, she looked at the newspapers he had just picked up; mellow and obliging.

She muttered a *hard bitch* at the fact of Alma Morgan being childless by design, a *bloody heathen* because she had become an atheist, a *cold cow* at her having written only once to thank her school-fee benefactress.

The witness stand, Molly read, was taken by a retired nurse, one who had once worked at the Dr. Barnster Home for Christian Waifs where Alma Morgan had spent her childhood. She told of two violent incidents involving the accused. Under cross-examination she agreed that violence had been common among the resident children, but asserted that Morgan's incidents were outstanding enough to still be fresh in her memory twenty years later.

Molly shook her head.

Another witness was the ex-principal of Wellington House, a boarding school for girls. She recounted the time when Alma Morgan, aged fifteen, had pushed her non-swimmer scholastic rival into the swimming pool's deep end when the two of them were the only people present. Examined by counsel for the defence, the principal admitted that the only proof of this having happened was the word of the rival, who, yes, had survived.

Even so, Molly thought, tutting.

A teacher presently employed at Barnster told under oath of a recent conversation with Alma Morgan. The accused had said, in reference to her husband, that one of these days she was going to kill him. The teacher remained unshaken by the defence's cross-examination.

"Guilty as hell," Molly sentenced handsomely.

The driver swung his head. "You what?"

"This bleeding murderess down in Exeter. Deserves to get her neck stretched. Not fit to live, rubbish like that. Ought to be put out of circulation permanently, evil animal that it is. A tooth for a tooth, I say."

When she had done with more condemnations, each with a soothing lack of originality, a glut of the familiar,

Molly read through reports of the trial in other newspapers. At length she turned to the much more interesting kidnapping case. She felt eased but not satisfied.

Contrary to popular opinion, an opinion popular on account of its assumption of decency, if executions were public in the West they would be extremely well attended. The next best thing is sitting in on a murder trial as an observer. People of high or low degree, of obscurity or fame, they repeatedly suffer tedium and discomfort in order to attend a capital case and savour its high points, and only a courageous small percentage would admit to being there out of blood lust.

Donald ached thoroughly. Marathon runner breasts the tape, he hurt all over, toe to jaw. As he moved inside the courtroom with the others at that curious, fast, knee-lifting shuffle of a crowd alerted to fun ahead or danger behind, he nodded his relief continually.

For two hours Donald had waited in the corridor, fifteenth in line. The floor was unrelenting marble, he was too far from the wall for leaning.

His sole consolation had been pleasure disguised as amusement in the way people looked at him. Donald could tell they thought they were seeing a celebrity, a novelist or actor or something, who was covering the trial incognito.

He wore flannels, a blazer, dark glasses, a hat. The last pair, coupled with his moustache, would, he knew, make him unrecognisable to everybody except the one for whom he was taking this fantastic risk.

At this stage of the scheme, Donald felt, he could do nothing finer for his wife than show himself to her, let her see that he was behind her all the way. He just hoped she wouldn't cry out when she saw him, or burst into tears, or gasp his name, or in some other form destroy everything he had worked so hard to create. That she lacked his own cool nerve was undeniable.

The decision to attend the trial Donald had made in his sleeping bag this morning, suddenly. It came to him out of nowhere, he was convinced. He would have been splutter indignant at any suggestion that the venture had been behind his move to the Exeter area yesterday.

Thrilled at the idea of being able to give even more to his wife and the scheme than living rough, eating poor food and braving every kind of foul weather, he had scuffled his feet about like a horizontal gig.

Not long after that Donald had been standing outside a clothing store when its owner came to open up. The expense he would cover with another stamp sale. Clothing he would destroy, no small gesture, that, in itself.

Donald had a niggle about being here in court, but, as he frequently mentioned to himself, he wasn't going to let it get him down. The niggle was that he would have no way of proving afterwards, scheme exposed, that he had in fact executed this outrageous venture.

In the public gallery Donald got a good seat, second row. He could see everything and, more important, could himself be seen, was in clear view of the dock.

Looking around, Donald established counsel, both for the defence and for the prosecution. Head of the latter, Peter Wembley, young and vigorous enough to score a touchdown, had close-cropped blond hair to go with a pink complexion. He was the type, Donald thought happily, who got believed whatever he said because he looked so clean and English.

Next Donald took in the press section. He picked out

two men he had seen before, one of whom had taken his photograph outside the Old Bailey during the Gosport trial.

With surprise, Donald remembered that Henry Gosport was dead. It seemed foggy to Donald now, that scene in his den when he fired the shot, foggier yet those other scenes which came afterwards, the preparation and departure. Everything had gone so smoothly.

Too smoothly?—was the following thought. It made Donald feel, strangely, as though he were trapped. It made him wonder if his being here could be part of a vast, complex conspiracy. It made him think that at any second everyone in court would slowly, slowly turn to face him— and his trial for the murder of Henry Gosport would begin.

Made uneasy by confused emotions, the major pair amounting to yearning and fear, Donald sat in a shrivel until the prisoner was brought in. Backed by a guard of either sex, she stood side-on to the public gallery, her hands resting lightly on the dock's ledge.

With his wife's entry Donald entered a different emotional field. He was prickly that Alma looked so well, unusually attractive even in her best tailored suit and with her hair done by a professional.

Reversewise, Donald expected Alma would think him greatly changed. She would be able to see on him the signs of strain, his ordeal's ravages.

As he began to make discreet movements to draw his wife's attention, Donald grew a measure drastic about the eyes. He felt vaguely offended.

Court opened.

Time passed and Alma continued to look almost nowhere but at judge or witness, jury or counsel. That Donald gradually eased off on his attention-catching movements was due not to the conclusion that they were a waste of time—she wasn't going to look around—rather because his fidgets had started his immediate neighbours glancing and chafing.

A psychiatrist took the witness stand. Not once did Alma budge her eyes from him during his testimony and examination. Only when it had been established to everybody's total satisfaction that the prisoner was sane and always had been did she relent, look away, look around the whole room.

Her gaze reached Donald—and went straight past. His shot-up hand was too late to make a catch. He told himself not to worry, there would be other chances.

With the psychiatrist gone there was a boring stretch during which counsel and judge discussed a point of law that Donald didn't understand. He jiggled one leg. He became quietly outraged on seeing a man further along the row from him begin on the furtive eating of a sandwich.

The next witness to be called, to Donald's shock, was his mother. By way of defence he smirked, tough guy can take it, for nothing was happening as envisioned and his emotions were being assaulted.

Small, jaw like a brow, wearing her usual dark and outdated clothes, though her hat was patently new, Mrs. James Morgan took the stand as though it were the wheelhouse of a storm-battered ship she had come to save.

Sworn in, she told via answers to questions of the awful life her war-hero son had led with his wife, detailing the rows and the physical damage he had always tried to hide and his tears. She told about her daughter-in-law's cruel tongue and bossy manner. Unasked, she told of her conviction, long held, that sooner or later one of Alma Morgan's jealous rages would end in tragedy.

Remembering those rows, remembering especially one that scored a black eye (won when the door he slammed bounced back on him), not remembering any tears but knowing how bad his memory could be, Donald felt abused. Once more his eyes turned drastic.

The defence took its turn. Donald breathed tightly through his nose to help the witness when she was cross-examined by John Randolph Whitehall, who anyone could see was an incompetent, an old failure who should have retired long ago.

Help was unneeded by Mrs. James Morgan, who repulsed in imperious style as though defence counsel had crept up from below stairs. Without so much as a flicked glance at the dock, she reviled her daughter-in-law. Her son she spoke of glowingly, making Donald sway to his feeling of being petted and wanted and appreciated.

After that witness had left, the proceedings became dull again. Someone in the courtroom somewhere produced a yawn so loud it was trailed by titters. Peter Wembley rubbed his eyes. Jurors took to looking at the high windows.

On Donald, at a creep, came the urge to bring matters to an end; now. Maybe the scheme didn't need to go any further than this, he reasoned hesitantly, its point having as good as been made. He could announce that he was alive.

How he could do it was, he mused, he could stand up and call out an order for silence, and then with everyone staring at him he could take off his hat, take off his dark glasses, and say in a ringing voice, "I am Donald Morgan." Or perhaps preface with, "May I introduce myself?"

With the urge to end it came excitement. Donald's heart started to thump unevenly, despite him seeing the act as sensible, he believed, not as having far more drama and immediacy than a later announcement.

There was still nothing happening in court.

Donald had not yet decided whether or not to make a move when he began to make one. He got to his feet. The floorboards gave up a rumble. Neighbours and several others elsewhere in the courtroom looked around.

Heart noisy, chest tight, Donald stared at his wife in willing her to turn this way. She remained intent on what the judge had to say. Again acting before a decision, Donald started to move along the row, on his way out.

Managing to keep his yawn quiet, not one like that yowl this morning from the man beside him, Bran mused: And they took me off the Northwood business for this.

His complaint, however, was made more in amusement than ire. The trial, he admitted, was not all that bad, just standard fare, predictable and bland, though for Dear Reader he had managed to turn yesterday's sharp exchange between rival lawyers into a furious shouting match.

Savingly, there was the centrepiece herself, Bran allowed. While as sparse in colour and dash as anyone else connected with the trial, Alma Morgan did have an undoubted presence. What it consisted of was far from plain. But, in spite of what the psychiatrist had stated, Bran thought that the basic essence could be insanity.

The prisoner showed no fear or worry, only at times an intensity of her acute awareness, such as when Dr. Hazlett had given his opinion. The impression was of somebody who believed in miracles. She seemed to have convinced herself that no matter what happened, what was said, what proofs were shown, the jury was going to find her not guilty.

Which, being so convinced, would make her as unique as Brandon Peel, Bran thought. Everyone else, police or press, law or lay, knew that Alma Morgan would be the third woman to hang in Britain this year.

Bran looked across at defence counsel. Poor old Whitehall. Tomorrow the trial would end and his hour in the relative big time would be over. Worse, he would have failed. But that was not entirely the fault of his talent. Only the finest, most celebrated, most expensive advocate, who in addition had gone to Eton with the judge's son, could have hoped to get Alma Morgan off with life imprisonment. The nation wouldn't stand for such a calm unrepentant lady escaping the noose after shooting dead her clean, straight, hard-working, non-smoking, non-drinking, God-fearing husband, a man who had spent six years fighting for his country.

Why hadn't the prisoner been coached?—Bran questioned sighingly. Any lawyer worth his salt would have had his client wringing her hands, wiping her eyes at every mention of her dead spouse, making the occasional outburst to protest her innocence. There was no business like show business. If you wanted to be a star or beat a rap or sell a second-hand car, you had to put on a performance.

Bran snared another yawn inside his mouth. That didn't prevent an epidemic. A good half of the twenty-odd reporters produced shivery yawns, dogs waiting for the meat.

Dutiful, Bran sat on through testimony by police—a sergeant, a constable and two detectives. It was all solidly incriminating. He left at a sidle during the swearing-in of a ballistics man, who would close the day.

After an offensive sandwich in one of those milk bars where they seemed unaware of war's end and quality's rebirth, Bran drove out of town. He went to Morgan Orchards.

The door was opened by the victim's mother, hatless. She said, "If you're a journalist—good-bye."

"I am, but—"

"You're the eleventh in two days and I have nothing to say to you."

"I'm Brandon Peel of the *Standard*," Bran said. "Did you happen to see this morning's edition, ma'am?"

With a switch in attitude from dire to pleasant, Mrs. James Morgan asked, " 'Born a Victim'?"

Bran nodded. His interview in quotes with Donald Morgan had been subbed from strident to crippled and stressed the valiant soldier. "I wrote it."

"Come in, do."

Bran got tea and cake, his thigh patted, a tour of the house ending in its attic, a recent photograph of Donald Morgan. That the woman who had spoken so shrewishly and damagingly in court was a charmer depressed him.

Giving Bran a further push into the black was his need to repeatedly lie, if only with a smile, every time Mrs. Morgan returned happily to the alleged fact that the visitor had had a nice long talk with her deceased son.

Bran still didn't get cheerful when, as he was taking his leave, three other reporters arrived in a shared taxi, only to be denied an interview.

Back in Exeter, rain falling, Bran went to the cinema rather than go to the bar where he knew he would find the company of colleagues. He wasn't in the mood.

Next day in court Bran was taken away from himself by the natural pull of crescendo. The ambience had a creak. While everybody looked alert, many also looked as though they hoped they didn't, not if it meant stamping them as vindictive.

The evidence was all in before eleven o'clock. The time had come to sum up. Peter Wembley did so for the Crown in masterly fashion, honest in his avoidance of histrionics, clever in his refusal to gaudify Alma Morgan as a monster.

The accused was a woman whose demeanour demonstrated only too clearly her belief that she had the right to play God, the barrister said. She felt free of competition, being an atheist. This attitude could be contagious. The very fabric of society was threatened by the existence of people like Alma Morgan. The death sentence, therefore, was vitally necessary, not simply as a triumph of Christian justice, but also to stop that rot of self-granted omnipotence from spreading.

When Peter Wembley sat down, the courtroom's hiss/ murmur/sigh was like applause, an acclaim rendered all the more potent by its restraint.

In a nearby pub, standing up among a crush to eat plates of cottage pie, the press agreed that betting on the trial's outcome would be a waste of time, since Morgan was obviously going to swing. Even an attempt to get up a lottery on how long your twelve good men and true would be out came to nothing.

While outwardly no more sensitive about the affair than his colleagues, while using "that hard bitch" nearly as often as anyone else, Bran felt amiss in his private self.

Thief with a conscience, he was not amused. He reckoned he was being influenced either by the bourgeois background he thought he had buried long ago, or by the suspicion that Alma Morgan could be innocent. On the whole, he preferred the former's weakness to the latter's stupidity.

Or again, Bran thought when he was back in court after the lunch break, could be he was pulling for the loser. Poor Whitehall, who now had his turn at summing up. In his wig and gown he looked like something time's dog had dragged in from the seventeenth century, having lost weight, his wig sometimes moving when he spoke and the gown ready to fall off. Yet a certain hardness in his face kept him from being pathetic, your man about failure. He even attained a measure of arrogance as he talked of circumstantial evidence, of Alma Morgan's fingerprints not being found anywhere in connexion with the crime— gun, shells, vase, kiln, shovel.

When John Randolph Whitehall leapt to stature, on finishing a review of events, it happened so unexpectedly that for a moment there was almost no change in the court's semi-apathy.

"That is the official brief," Whitehall said, surveying the jury. "And one which I am professionally bound to offer. As a man and not a barrister, however, I do not believe Alma Morgan's story for a moment."

Straightening to tautness, Bran scanned about. People were changing position as though remembering what they should be doing instead of sitting here. Jurymen looked at each other, deaf seek the wink of jovial conspiracy. Peter Wembley and team, they drew on smiles grim enough to frighten off the biggest of gift horses. Like a hibernator emerging too early from some grey thicket, the old judge's face tic'd and blinked his uncertainty.

Alma Morgan had folded her arms. Over them she was holding her head at a downward slant while staring from the angle as if she had spectacles on the end of her nose. It was not a pleasant stare. The barrister made no attempt to return it as he went on to elaborate his shock statement.

The struggle for possession of the gun between Mr. and Mrs. Morgan had never happened. Alma Morgan was lying. The truth must be that the prisoner was protecting someone she loved. She was prepared to do so even if it meant losing her life. She was that kind of person.

To Bran's relief, John Randolph Whitehall had the wit to keep his assertion not only free of gesturing and sonorous melodrama, but short. When he sat down, and the judge prepared to give his directions to the jury, it was amid a mumble of comment which had a tang of approval.

Although the new slant had small hope of influencing the trial's outcome, Bran knew, it did introduce a needed element of chance—as well as making for excellent copy. The odd response of Alma Morgan, who had now gone back to normal, he would describe as a glow of hope.

The judge spoke, a model of concision.

When the jury left, it had been directed to bring in a verdict of either not guilty, giving total freedom, or guilty, the sentence to be execution, no other possibilities being acceptable to the court.

His lordship retiring, everyone got up to go, to fill in time until the twelve men signalled readiness.

In the pub, present was only a distant cousin of the tension Bran had experienced in other cases at this juncture, a drive not unlike violence kept under control by force. No one was wary. Some of the reporters played darts.

While sipping beer and nibbling the crust off a meat pie whose contents he didn't trust, Bran wondered if John Randolph Whitehall was in love with Alma Morgan. He fantasised about the lawyer himself being the phantom lover he had offered by way of freak defence—an act of legal desperation if ever there was one, that.

After an hour and a half word came of the jury's imminent return. Leaving the pub, the reporters went back to court taking deep last drags on cigarettes.

Everyone settled. The jury came in. Asked if they had reached a verdict acceptable to them all, the foreman said they had. Asked what it was, he said guilty.

The courtroom was silent. His lordship looked at the base of the dock in asking, "Alma Morgan, do you have anything to say before sentence is passed upon you?"

"I do not."

The judge fumbled as he tried to be efficient at putting on over his wig the square of black cloth called a cap. Bran didn't look at Alma Morgan until the judge did.

She stood straight, almost at attention, though without rigidity, her manner more relaxed than that of her guards. She gazed upon his lordship as though he were about to give her a citation, or invite her to the banquet, or turn into a handsome young prince.

Insane, yes, was the thought that came quietly to Bran. It came again when Alma Morgan sent the old man a nod, teacher encourages hesitant pupil.

"Prisoner at the bar," the judge said, firm but not happy. "You have been found guilty of wilful murder. The sentence of the court upon you is that you be taken from this place to a lawful prison, and thence to a place of execution, and that there you suffer death by hanging, and that your body be buried within the precincts of the prison in which you shall have been last confined before your execution." He looked away. "May the Lord have mercy on your soul."

FIVE

The condemned cell was no more bleak than the basement apartment of a bachelor who hated frills and fuss, loved spartan cleanliness.

A large, elongated room smelling of carbolic soap, with whitewashed walls and two high windows purblinded by frosted glass, it had several pieces of simple furniture—chairs both straight and easy, twin beds under bright covers, two tables, wardrobe, foot locker, shelf of books. The adjoining bathroom might also have belonged to that bachelor, fixtures standard, if it had owned a door.

Alma quickly got used to the place. Within days she felt she had been resident for weeks, just as she felt in that same time that she had known them for months, her eight guards, the uniformed wardresses who were always with her in pairs, a change made every six hours.

The food was better than before. It came not from the prison kitchen but the staff canteen, for, as was pointed out to Alma, they could hardly send separate meals for guards and prisoner, they wouldn't have the face.

And yes, she was answered briskly when she asked, in three weeks time she could order whatever she wanted, within reason, for her last breakfast.

Alma slipped smoothly into the routine. She was as-
sisted by her quiet relish for the situation. More so than
before, she felt proud as well as privileged, bearable arrogance and cheery humility living together in her without
shame. This, she knew—everything from the time of the
policemen coming to the house—would be the greatest
experience of her life, as the war was for Donald.

The routine was sleep, eat, exercise yard, talk or games,
eat, nap, more cards or dominoes, yard again (solo as
before), radio or talk or solitude, eat, letters to read and
answer, books and bed.

With time passing by her as swiftly as it did, Alma was
never bored. Rather, she hoarded every moment of these
her golden days, though she sometimes had to remind
herself to do so, to turn her back on some petty irritation
and grow up again into her pride.

Visitors were few. Apart from John Randolph Whitehall and prison officials, there was only the chaplain. Re-
quests for visits did come in, from a farmer neighbour,
two old schoolmates, a spiritualist, the girl she had once
shared a flat with, but Alma saw no sense in entertaining
people whose motives were suspect, they having ignored
her until now.

The prison chaplain was a young man with outstuck
ears and a thin neck. He seemed to take encouragement
from Alma's vagueness in response to his plaintive, "Perhaps I can bring you back into the arms of Jesus." She
didn't have the hard to tell him he was wasting his time.

Alma had two worries, which she secretly enjoyed and
brought out to examine sternly during idle breaks.

First there was her husband. She couldn't help think,
disloyal though it made her feel, that Donald might spoil
what was going magnificently through one of his sponta-

neous acts of folly. Almost, and this made her feel so stupid that she'd had no room for the disloyalty emotion, she had expected him to come walking into court to proclaim his existence.

The Appeal against her sentence, an attempt to have it reduced to life imprisonment, was Alma's other worry. John Randolph Whitehall had become slink-eyed to such a degree, possibly out of mortification at having failed in the trial, that she was unable to tell if his confidence was false when he talked of her Appeal.

If it did by some chance succeed and she was reprieved, Alma knew the scheme would be drastically sapped in potency if not outright ruined. Naturally people would say, See, in the end the innocent never hang.

With the eight wardresses, innocence or guilt was not brought up. Their charge they treated like a juvenile delinquent, even though they were mostly about her own age. Ranging in build from sturdy to fat, they had all been in the armed forces and on occasion got into hissed tribal arguments, forgetting Alma, once to the extent that she spent fifteen minutes in the bathroom before they realised she was missing.

The eight were all married or divorced, all childless, all with little good to say about their husbands. Alma's impression was that they believed she had been treated harshly for years by Donald yet had declined to state it out of feminine propriety. While sympathising, they made it clear that in their opinion she deserved her punishment, although that, the gallows, was another matter which never came into the talk.

The women made the best of it for all concerned in respect of their constant attendance, the death watch whose major purpose was to prevent suicide. The law said that the life of a condemned felon must not be given, freely, but taken, with force.

Alma was steadying along, supported by her conviction that the cause was just. She allowed almost nothing to bring her low in spirit, could even find amusement in the sewer press articles nominally written by people she barely remembered: "I Dated A Murderess," "My School Chum Became A Killer."

But beyond the first few days after conviction the case dwindled in the newspapers, a final shot being a photograph of the victim.

It, Alma recognised, was the latest in a series of birth-day pictures Donald had had taken all his adult life at the behest, and expense, of his mother. The photographer had made his subject look so charming and angelic, so in need of protection, that Alma couldn't help but be filled with respect for her mother-in-law's cunning.

It rains more in Ireland than in Wales, more in Wales than in Scotland, more in Scotland than in England, and more in England than in Ireland. Or so they would have you believe in the tourist offices of Cardiff, Glasgow, Man-chester and Dublin. The truth is that wherever you go thereabouts, it rains, professionally. If it didn't, Eire would not be green, Wales would suffer unbearable over-crowding through lack of emigration, Scotland would have no stag or grouse, whiskey or salmon, and the En-glish would have nothing to talk about. It rains.

Donald was sick to death of it. If there was anything worse than sitting chill and damp in a tiny tent, alone, staring out at a desertion made more desolate by millions of raindrops, he would have been interested in hearing about it.

He decided on escape.

Leaving his tent where it stood rather than go through the chore of dealing with sodden canvas, which would then have to be carried, he set off with all his other possessions packed in the knapsack.

As far as Donald was presently concerned, if anyone wanted to steal that tent, they were most welcome. He marched with spirits rising to the nearest hostel.

It was full.

Donald tramped on around the rim of Exeter. He was dripping and grumpy, his sunken spirits all the worse for his previous thoughts of being drily and warmly indoors among girls with creased, skimpy shorts, advising people on routes, talking of politics and the Orchard Murder, having snacks.

The next hostel being full also—German cyclists—Donald waited for and then boarded a bus that would take him to Exeter's inner suburbs. Several times he asked himself just who had won the war anyway.

Off the bus Donald squelched to a commercial hotel, brief home of lorry drivers, salesmen for dubious firms and couples with questionable bona fides. The reception clerk looked at him in doubt.

He said, "I don't know if we have a vacancy."

Donald, dripping loudly on the linoleum, was close to having a lump in his throat. All thoughts of future glory had gone from his mind.

He blurted, "You don't know who I am."

The man shook his head. "No."

After having a sharp word with himself, Donald explained that he was Sir Percy Rangeway, the property dealer, travelling incognito. The clerk showed him where to sign.

His room, post-tent, was a place of luxury. He gazed about in gladness while stripping. The bed was so soft he took sixty instead of his intended five.

After a bath along the hall Donald dressed in his new clothes, the blazer and flannels. He had kept them because he would have to look decent, didn't want to be in hiking gear, when he made his triumphant entrance into the public eye, a man come back from the grave.

Down in the lobby, lounging before a coal fire, bright, Donald browsed through periodicals with his eyebrows raised. He was jolted, and delighted, to find in a three-day-old newspaper a photograph of himself.

On settling to admiration Donald told himself he had been quite right, psychic some might say, to come to this particular locale. The matter he left there, as he sensed there was nowhere else it could be taken, in comfort.

When Donald went out for a bite of supper, preferring a lively restaurant to the hotel's quiet dining room, he left the open newspaper behind rather than take it along. He considered the move shrewd, shrewder even than not tearing out the photograph as a keepsake.

Later that night, while shaving off his moustache (it had become a bore), Donald thought of his mother. She had entrusted the most recent picture of her dead soldier hero son exclusively to her favourite newspaper, the accompanying copy said. Donald thought of how deeply she must be grieving. He wondered should he telephone her to divulge the truth.

Not caring what anyone might think, twice a day Molly went to the newsagent's for papers. Not only that, each time she did she bought several different ones, which she took brisk-furtive home, where she scanned pages with care. Always she was irked.

What made her so was that she never found the expected: something on the Orchard Murder. There was not a word. The story had come to an end. Nothing more was left to be said.

Why the story hadn't ended for Molly, she knew, why it continued to rankle more than interest, was because of the gradual assemblage formed involuntarily by her mind of certain facts. This had started when she had read the defence opinion that Alma Morgan was protecting someone she loved.

The result of the assemblage could have formed a question, had Molly been inclined to ask it. She preferred to own a rankle, as, for one thing, the question was the kind of stuff you saw on television crime series.

Coincidence or non-substance was of course behind the disturbing facts: that Henry had not been seen since the exact same day a body was destroyed in the Morgan Orchards kiln; that for Henry to go this long without making contact, if only with his son, was outlandish; that his common-law wife frequently got the dulling conviction that he was dead, which had never happened to her before; that he fitted perfectly with the description of Anglo-Saxon male thirty to forty years old and above average in height; that he too had broken his right collar bone and left tibia; that applied also those other facts from when her question had been, Did Henry kill Donald Morgan?

With every day that passed without word from her man, Molly grew stronger in her determination not to ask, Did Mr. and Mrs. Morgan kill Henry Gosport when he came to extort money on the grounds that those who bore false witness should be made to pay for it?

Someone was sweeping up the broken glass, doing so without the mouth of importance. Sand had long since been spread to cover the blood. Technicians, investigators and all police had gone with the exception of a lone constable. People behind the ropes were starting to drift away, there being no new arrivals for them to explain matters to, after coaxing.

Bran left reluctantly. He always did. The scene of a crime had for him more fascination than it did for John Average, he knew, though less than for a policeman, whose love of violence was due in part to his job having turned out to be nine-tenths bland routine, not the full-time excitement he had expected, for love feeds on what it misses.

Blasé Bran might pretend to be, even to himself, but a scene's bustle and throb, everyone's urgency, the clamour of movement, they never failed to fill him with nervous stimulation. Leaving was like watching a circus pack up.

With a man from the *Mirror* Bran went to a milk bar, where over coffee they got an extra half hour out of the event: a jewellery shop smash-and-grab, raiders shoot dead a youth who tries to interfere, wound a bystander, knock down and kill a woman in driving off.

Outside again, *Mirror* man gone, Bran set out to find where he had left his car. As he walked he realised, with a curious lift, that he was close to the Stepney area. He quickened his step. His mild dejection had faded.

A quarter hour later Bran was in Can Lane, knocking at the door of number 10. He did so while watching the curtains. They twitched. Nothing else happening, he knocked again, harder. The curtains parted like a cloth ripped up the middle.

Behind the glass Molly Harker glared, mouthing, "You."

Loudly Bran said, "That's right."

"What you want?"

Still loud: "What's that?"

Molly Harker went from sight. Next, the door opened, all of two inches. From the slice of face came, "There's no need to raise the whole street."

"Hello. I called before once, a while ago."

"And now you're calling again."

"I thought we might go out for a drink."

"Don't know why you thought that," Molly Harker said. "There's no news value in me or mine."

"I wasn't thinking about business," Bran said. "I just thought we could have a friendly drink."

"Sure you did."

"We could drive to some nice pub somewhere."

"You press boys're only after one thing, and it's not the usual one."

"What's the usual one?"

"Get off it, mate."

"Anyway," Bran said, "this is personal. I'm not inter-ested in Henry Gosport."

"He's not here even if you are."

"On holiday still?"

"No, he's gone to have a natter with the Pope."

"Why don't you open the door?" Bran said, bolder be-cause of the gangster's absence.

Molly Harker said, "This is wide enough." Her eye looked at him steadily. It blinked several times before the abrupt, "Don't you think there's something funny about that Orchard thing?"

Bran jerked out, "What?"

"Oh, nothing."

He leaned closer. "If you mean Alma Morgan's manner—"

"I don't."

"—it's because she's insane, in my opinion."

"Rotten piece of goods, more like."

"How about that drink?"

"Busy," Molly Harker said. "Good-bye. And don't call again." The door closed.

"It's the hottest June in years, I've heard."

"This is the best campsite in Devonshire."

"You may think otherwise, but I think the rise in income tax is a scandal."

"The Orchard Murder? Sorry, I don't go to the pictures much nowadays."

"Anyone who thinks this is hot doesn't know what he's on about, he ought to have seen summers in the old days."

"I see where they got them smash-and-grabbers."

"Pity there's no decent campsites in this county."

"Yes, that Morgan woman's going to get topped right enough, and justly so, shooting down her man Roland like a dog."

Donald had many conversations as he strolled among the tents and caravans, or stood waiting his turn at the tap, or borrowed a spot of milk. He loved knowing that in every single case the other person, within a week or so, was going to gasp, "I met him! We were this close!"

Donald would miss that and the company when he moved to the quiet spot he had already chosen, from where he would make his triumphant emergence.

It was all planned. It had become Donald's favourite

reverie. What he particularly liked was the flash-forward of himself walking in on his mother—after word had been given elsewhere but before it had reached Morgan Orchards.

Far better to wait, Donald had finally decided, than break the news to her earlier, by telephone, or even to pave the way via the ruse of calling as a medium who knew from contacts on the other side that her son wasn't there. Better and safer. Mother could do something scatty and give the game away.

The secret was best left in his own capable hands, Donald reminded himself whenever he got a tinge of guilt over his mother's needless grieving. In order not to be tempted to give in at such times (old softy that he was), he sought distraction by finding people to talk to. They didn't have to be interesting. Standing there, fanning himself with his hat, he drew pleasure from knowing how much he was giving them, how excited they were going to be with their future gasp of, "I met him!"

It was not until she discovered that she had no concern about the Appeal's outcome, was unworried that it might succeed, that Alma suspected herself of being kept under permanent sedation.

One whole day she spent slipping to and fro between scoff and conviction. The former weakened following supper when she sat listening for the third time to the story of little Mabel's tonsillectomy. She wasn't bored. She ought to have been bored.

Children's illnesses Alma found excruciatingly uninteresting at the best of times. The best of times this could well be, in a sense, but no matter how high her spirits climbed she could not possibly, she knew, listen in a normal frame of mind complacently even once to a woman tell every bead of her daughter's calvary.

The nightcap cocoa was brought, three mugs on a tray. What Alma hadn't noted before was that one of the mugs was a darker blue than the others. It was the one she was handed, she, as usual, being served first.

Out of usual was Alma's, "I think I'll sit over there to drink it."

That would be all right, the guards indicated. They stayed on at the table, one reading, the other doing crochet, neither attentive to their charge.

At the room's other end Alma sat on the farthest bed, facing the bathroom doorway one yard distant and with her back to the guards. After making several arm-lifts as if sipping she got casually up and, not looking behind, strolled into the bathroom. She flushed her cocoa away and returned to the main room with the mug by her spine.

She slept soundly.

On awakening, remembering, Alma felt a mite foolish for her suspicion of being sedated yet decided to persist if only because she had gained such enjoyment out of her cocoa-ridding ruse—and was there not significance in that?

Being a model prisoner, one who had never given her guards a second's alarm, Alma again had no trouble in smuggling liquids into the bathroom. She got rid of her orange juice and tea, ate the solids. Later she did the same with elevenses.

As far as she herself was concerned, Alma felt no different. She had almost forgotten the matter until one of the wardresses asked, gruff, "Not up to scratch today, Morgan?"

"Headache."

"I'll get you something for it."

"Oh no, thank you," Alma said hastily. "I'll just lie down for a while."

"It's the Appeal, probably," the woman said. "The suspense of waiting to see how it turns out."

"I dare say you're right."

"Tell you what."

"Yes?"

"Why not have a nice lie-down?"

In time, Alma was able to prevent herself from answering that she had just said that, which would have been unlike the person they were used to, as well as bad manners.

She smiled. "Good idea."

While lying on her bed, looking about at her surroundings, listening to the two women exchange desultory talk, thinking on the situation, Alma accepted that yes, she patently had been on a course of sedatives.

How could she otherwise have seen this place as anything other than sordid? How could she have thought these dull, bossy women bright and friendly? How had she been able to treat her circumstances so lightly?

Thereafter Alma became progressively more edgy and despondent, although she did manage to get nowhere close to imagining things going wrong, Donald being ill.

It was following an afternoon visit from the chaplain, whose sanctimonious simper she found repellent, that Alma reached her limit. She wanted no more of straight reality, of a world viewed through uncoloured glasses.

To the next pair of guards to come on duty she explained that her lack of vitality must be caused by hunger, since she had thrown up most of her breakfast and lunch.

The glance exchanged between wardresses did not go un-seen. Food and drink came quickly, and as quickly got consumed.

An hour later Alma was playing dominoes with her guards and smiling at their chatter of domestic doings.

Big Ben was striking. The deep, rich, spaced beats seemed to Molly to be like punches in the back from someone who loved you. Passingly, she forgot what she was waiting to hear, recalled how in wartime people used to listen every night, like this, to Big Ben's chimes as they preceded the nine o'clock news. It had been a solemn few seconds. Instead of yourself you thought of others: the sons and fathers and husbands who had died and whose women had died inside, and those to whom it was hap-pening right now, thousands of them with each deep throbbing cry of the bell. Still today, years later, if a radio was playing in public and the chimes came on, people paused, softened, looked away from one another, perhaps remembered a voice they were beginning to forget.

Molly felt a tightening in her throat, which she thought soft of her, she having lost no one in the war. She sniffed alert as the ninth beat lingered away into silence.

The news began.

There was nothing in the headlines, which was fair enough, Molly granted in her generous way. The affair had never been all that big in the first place.

Patiently Molly listened to word of politics and strikes, deaths and disasters, cricket and tennis, understanding maybe a third of what she heard and of that being inter-ested in possibly a tenth. She looked dartingly at the radio to listen to the man tell that the Appeal had failed, that

Alma Morgan would be executed as scheduled in three days.

Molly switched the radio off. She had an odd feeling of vicious satisfaction.

There was a white five-barred gate in the hedge. Beyond it a field rose gently to a crest on which grew a huge elm. Under the tree a tent was pitched.

Pretty as a picture, Donald pronounced, mostly by way of self-congratulation. He had paused at the gate on the second-class road to look up and admire his camping spot.

Purists would condemn him for having made camp in so dangerous a place, Donald knew (crest would catch the wind, tree could fall), just as he recognised the risk of the farmer sending policemen to eject a trespassing camper; but he had been unable to resist, the site had so much charm, it was going to look wonderful in the press photographs. Every detail helped.

Climbing the gate (it was openable but he felt youthful when doing the climb) Donald went on up the field. He plodded. It had been a long hike to the village and back, for today's newspapers.

If you asked Donald, there had been altogether too much hiking. He was glad that, now the Appeal was out of the way, a safe failure, he was free to end his month-long ordeal, emerge into the light, which he would bring about tomorrow afternoon, to catch the late editions.

When Donald stopped midway up the incline, as far as he was concerned it was for him to have another appreciative view of the campsite, not to give his slaving lungs a rest. To prove it he smiled all the broader.

In his tent, boots off, recovered, Donald went through the newspaper reports again. They were on page two or three, with further back still mention of the usual minor agitations by various anti–capital punishment groups.

While he told himself how pleased he was about the Appeal failing, Donald felt low, which he distantly admitted to and vaguely blamed on the relative obscurity of the press reports, certainly not on the fact that they were all Alma Morgan, Alma Morgan, Alma Morgan, with never a word to say about her supposed victim.

At noon, morosing by the fire over a sandwich (the bread was dry), Donald was visited by inspiration. It stopped his jaw, straightened his back.

He would dispense with his amnesia excuse; with offering any excuse at all. He would admit to having perpetrated a fraud, which, of course, was an indictable offence. Undoubtedly he would go to jail. That would make him more of a martyr to the cause than he was already and place him ahead of his wife in the honour stakes.

None of this was acknowledged consciously by Donald beyond the excuse dispensing, which he thought he had decided on because, being an intelligent man, he realised how feeble the excuse of amnesia was. He guessed he must have known it all along, ever since Alma had put it forward, but had declined to recognise the fact out of misguided loyalty. He was like that.

Donald chewed on, nodding.

For much of the day, Alma felt fine. It had nothing to do with sedatives, she knew. It was the comfort of expectation. She waited from moment to moment for a prison official to bustle in with the news of Donald Morgan's return from the dead. The event, entry, would be made all the more intense by its contrast with yesterday's newsbreaking.

John Randolph Whitehall had looked like a man about to retire to bed for the last time, having walked a hundred miles in order to die at home.

He couldn't speak. It wasn't necessary. The two guards as well as Alma patted him by way of sympathy. He left without uttering a word, urged gently on his way by Alma, who, hurt by remorse on top of compassion, had the terrible temptation to gift him with the truth. She resisted. Revelation was Donald's chosen territory.

Glad the whole endeavour was nearly over, Alma had slept well. Her breakfast she consumed to the last crumb and drop, the while joking with her watchdogs, who looked strangely at her, this woman who had three days left to live.

What Alma looked at, and looked at, both at that time and later, was the door.

By four o'clock in the afternoon she had stopped feeling fine. She was exhausted. She was emotionally spent. She had intimations of hysteria and was no longer denying the possibility of the insane happening, of Donald not coming forward, being unable to—sick, lost on a moorland walk, trapped somehow somewhere, in a coma after an accident, stupefied on alcohol or drugs; dead.

Declining tea, Alma began to search for Donald's letter. It would prove beyond doubt that its author had been alive long after a skeleton was found in the kiln.

The wardresses watched in silence as Alma looked between and behind shelved books, scoured through the footlocker and rumpled through her clothes. It was when she grew more erratic, gasping, starting to drag the mattress off a bed, that the women rushed at her to take hold of an arm apiece.

Calm yourself, Morgan, they said with their faces loomed close. Take it easy.

"Let me go, please."

What are you looking for, they asked.

"A letter," Alma panted. She smiled to show how calm and rational she was. "A particular letter. One I got while I was on remand."

She was having a reaction to the bad news, they said.

"No no. That's all right. So am I. There's a letter I must get hold of."

They told her she should have drunk her tea.

"Why?"

They said tea was pleasant, soothing.

"I am perfectly fine, thank you. All I want is my letter."

She ought to have a nice glass of orange juice, they said.

Breathing through her nose, Alma nodded slowly. She said, "Look. I'll make a bargain with you. You find my letters and I'll drink your orange juice."

They said it would have to be the orange juice first.

"Quite."

The wardresses took Alma to a table, sat her down with humming sounds. One brought and watched her sip the drink while the other talked around the door to some-body outside.

The metal mug was empty when the somebody came back with the information that all correspondence from before, pre-conviction, had been burned.

Alma, happy to have the sedative's support, said she would like to see the warden to make an official statement.

A job well done, that was Bran's comment to himself about the piece he had just finished on the Camden Town bank robbery. He had made excitement out of what may have been the quietest caper on record: man walks in, whispers to teller he has a bomb, gets contents of till and walks out.

Bran was humming as he ambled along a corridor in the *Daily Standard* building on Fleet Street. Had he allowed himself to think about it he would have realised that he had done a lot of humming today.

His mind drifted to the evening ahead—a drink or three, a good feed, a look in on that cheeky redhead.

"Gangway!"

The call came from behind. Bran steered aside and told the bustler as he passed, "Don't you know you're supposed to yell, Hold the front page?"

The man looked back briefly to admonish, "This Suez thing's getting serious."

Happy to be indifferent to the sound of sabres rattling, Bran shrugged. He went back to his hum. When he broke off again it was to answer an hello from an approaching colleague, who next, having drawn level, halted with, "Right."

Bran also stopped. "Eh?"

"You were on the Orchard Murder, weren't you?"

"On it? Listen, that name—"

"Right," the man said deafly. "Well, the latest is that the Morgan woman claims the killing was a hoax. It never happened. Hubby is very much alive."

Bran felt cautious. He said, "Oh?"

The man, small and neat, prig face, told with glances at a sheet of yellow paper about a found skeleton and a plan to strike a blow for the anti–capital punishment lobby.

He ended, "Pathetic."

"Yes?"

"One of the oldest in the book. The only surprising thing is, she didn't try it sooner."

"What'll happen now?"

"Nothing, of course."

Leaning closer Bran asked an offended, "Won't there be some sort of enquiry?"

"Certainly not," the man said. "I don't even know if we're going to use this. Condemned people are forever making wild claims. This one isn't newsy."

"It couldn't be true, I don't suppose."

"But I think we can add it to the piece we do on Thursday, when the lady swings."

"Of course not."

"What?"

"I was wondering. Anything in it, you reckon?"

Flapping his sheet of yellow paper the man said, "Don't be thick, Greel."

"Peel."

"Right."

Bran said, "I think she must be out of her mind."

"The headshrinkers don't agree with you."

"A single psychiatrist."

"Either way, there's one teensy weensy detail the lady seems to have forgotten with her claim."

"Yes?"

"If the husband isn't dead," the man said, "where is he?" Smiling like a gifted punchliner he walked on.

Bran had neither smile nor hum as he made his way downstairs and out of the building. He was uneasy. He couldn't imagine Alma Morgan making a claim so wild and fictionesque, that was one scratcher of uneasiness. Another was, he could with no difficulty imagine her becoming involved in such a plan, her jib had that do-gooder cut.

Scratching also were the facts of Bran all along considering Alma Morgan to be either innocent or insane and of someone saying to him recently, "Don't you think there's something funny about that Orchard thing?"

Who that person was, Bran was unable to remember. He gave up the attempt as he strode along the street while not enquiring why he was striding.

Instead, he told himself sordidly that he was no more immune to drama's charm than anyone else, yokel, housewife, schoolchild, fool. He wanted nothing to interfere with his secret relish of the execution. Like many of those who professed opposition to or disgust over capital punishment he nevertheless wished to have a hanging carried out, wished it in a dank cave of the emotions, in order to feel in addition satisfyingly outraged, be able to look suitably aghast.

This was in Bran's mind while he was ostensibly thinking of drinks, feeds and cheeky redheads.

It was growing late in the Coach and Horses. The thin midweek crowd had started to get thinner yet, a sleeping dog was no longer in the way, and the barmaid, befuddled, held a finger under her nose while yawning.

Molly, quiet-nighting on beer, lit a cigarette and drifted on from the group of people she had joined minutes ago. She was sick to death of hearing about that stupid bank deal. You would think no one had ever pulled off a job before, the way folk went on and on and bloody on.

"Poor Morgan cow," Molly heard in nearing a table.

"It's only got itself to blame."

The pair of retired charwomen, spinsters, dressed to

dowdy by way of showing that although they might have had their moments they never did it for money, were six-Guinness solemn.

"She's against the noose, see," one said.

"They often is," the other gave back tartly, "them what's going to be topped."

"No, straight."

"It's a load of balls anyway."

"Oh, I know that."

Stopping, Molly asked, "What's all this, girls?" Her smile was imitation.

The women both talked at the same time, a clawed hand outstretched in a try at grasping full attention. Skilled in pub practice, Molly held her gaze somewhere between the two as she nodded half-lyingly at what she half-understood. She did get that the details were available on an inside page of the *Star* or maybe it was the *News*.

Going over to the bar Molly found damp, dispirited newspapers. She sought out the item. It was short. After reading quickly through Alma Morgan's claim she began on a slow reread while thinking, So this was how I find out Henry's dead, by reading a paper in the Coach.

There was no proof, but that had no interest for Molly. She accepted that the human remains in the orchard kiln belonged to her man, who had been put there by Donald and Alma Morgan after they had killed him.

Molly felt unusually, unpleasantly calm. Her cigarette she stubbed out with care before starting to read the item a third time, giving her eyes something to do while she thought about the Morgan woman going to swing for it and her husband letting her, so like a man, that, and about how difficult it would be to find Donald Morgan in order to kill him.

After folding the newspaper down with delicacy, curator pampers old manuscript, Molly said a placid goodnight to one and all, left the pub. She semi-recognised that she was purposely delaying her reaction to Henry's death, knowing the pain would be less cruel the farther she got from the event, and she counted herself lucky in having this important mission to keep her occupied meanwhile.

Pacing slowly along the grim-lit street Molly ignored a hesitant suggestion that Donald Morgan was undoubtedly in South America or somewhere else out of the question. He would be around Exeter, she insisted, in hiding.

Poor cow Alma had just twigged that Donald wasn't going to keep his part of the bargain, Molly pursued, though she had put up a dozen legitimate reasons for his non-appearance, and she could be right, he could still come forward, there was time yet. But appear or not, where would Hero be hidden?

It was when, after turning into Can Lane, Molly was discounting Donald Morgan's own attic as his hiding place, visualising the long room, that she got what her criminal's mind told her was sure to be the answer.

A tent. A tent like the one he had been playing with that time. By day he would be cycling around in full view, dressed like a scoutmaster; by night he would be sleeping in a tent among other summer campers.

Donald Morgan was findable in the extreme, Molly decided, because that was what she wanted. And once found he could be dealt with, probably not as soon as the law was going to deal with his missus, but soon enough.

Stimulated, a good deal less uncomfortably calm, Molly

swung around. On mental fingers she ticked off that she would telephone Sheffield Bill and have him bring a car to the house at once, back home get a gun and load it, alert Mrs. Brown to see to Johnny in the morning.

That was all the planning needed, Molly figured. She would set off straight away and drive through the night and start to search first thing. It was full speed ahead.

Molly had been striding. This she speeded up, broke step, went along the deserted street at a skip.

When Bran awoke, early, he thought he had a slight hangover. He allowed himself to whimper as he sat up and swivelled to get his feet on the floor. Sitting there rubbing stubble he ventured on the customary game of recreating the itinerary of the night before, starting this time with a beer after leaving the *Daily Standard* building.

Bran's hunch grew more acute when he realised he had no recollection of where else he had gone drinking. After that first Fleet Street pub—nothing. Covering, he went quickly to the bathroom.

Back again, kettle on for tea, Bran got the answer. There was nothing public for him to remember. Following the one beer he had come home. His pseudo-hangover was the result of a poor night's sleep.

Several factors had helped provoke insomnia, Bran acknowledged as he glared impatiently at the kettle. But, hapless parent to child, he told himself no, don't start. He didn't care to go through all that again, playing with those factors like building blocks, especially the cornerstone piece of Alma Morgan's face when the jury foreman had pronounced the verdict, an expression that could now be read as satisfaction.

Nevertheless, Bran pointed out, there was certainly a

farfetched chance of the woman's claim being true. The plot she outlined, was, as he had already seen, the kind of do-good thing that went with her type, which was another factor—and he had started.

Dressing with his back to the stove, having recalled that a watched kettle never boiled, Bran assured himself that factors or no factors, dreams of fantastic scoops notwithstanding, he was not about to set off driving down Exeter way, where he would have gone to see the mother-in-law, whose deadly evidence seemed, in retrospect, to have been peculiarly vindictive. He had more sense than that.

Anticipation is the finest of all human emotions. Leaving such as fear, anger and disgust to be enjoyed by the perverse or deranged, joy has a short life due to its own excess, surprise is recovered from amazingly fast, and love can cause stress if not hate.

But anticipation, being dread stood on its head, being hope in a less foolhardy coat, can linger indefinitely, most welcome, pleasuring with the word that whatever happens next it won't matter, nothing can change the now, this moment so dear.

Donald hummed. He couldn't remember when he had felt as fine. He had loved lounging in his sleeping bag for an extra hour this morning (normally he couldn't abide a lie-in), had loved preparing a special brunch, was loving this amble.

Hands afted, Donald idled along beside a hedge. It was out of sight of the road. Not that the road bothered him, a passing vehicle was rare enough, that tease he liked to save for when he was in the mood.

So it was nearly over, Donald mused, hamming a frown

to help him feel serious. All those weeks of strife and privation, rain and cold, poor meals, lodging in those awful commercial hotels with their cheap smell and those hostels filled with cloddish foreigners—over. The rest was gravy. Or rather, glory.

"Excuse me. May I introduce myself."

Or, "Hello. I'm Donald Morgan."

Or, "Pardon me. I believe you'll be interested in knowing who I am."

Donald shivered as through him coursed one of the tingles. He had been experiencing them since wakening, since realising that it was Christmas morning and Coronation Day and Bonfire Night and VE Day and Mardi Gras. This tingle made him stop on account of the way his knees twinged.

Grinning at full stretch, salesman clinching, Donald smoothed down his hair and ambled on. He swung his shoulders to replace the hum.

When, presently, he began to think plans, thinking of what came after he had changed into his new clothes, Donald felt the thoughts as an interruption. He left them. He knew precisely what he was going to do later. Or maybe later than that. Tonight. Tomorrow. The closer to the deadline the greater the impact, after all.

The official campsite consisted of a large field with its caravans and tents backed against the surrounding fence as though to get as far as possible from the stenchy waterless latrines in the middle.

Stooping, Molly peered inside a tent. It was empty apart from bedding and a pile of tinned foods. Straight again she moved on. She tried not to think of that tent being the right one, Morgan away somewhere, by hoping, not for the first time, that she didn't look too out of place in her city clothes. As if she gave a stuff.

In the next tent's entrance a woman sat knitting. From the way her eyes flitted all over the passing stranger Molly credited her with being the nosy-bitch type she could have approached, situation normal, to ask if a man fitting Morgan's description had been seen around. She couldn't ask; anyone. When you were going to kill somebody you didn't advertise that you were looking for him.

During the past hours, on needing to explain what was obviously a search, Molly had said she was seeking her cousin Mary—tall, fair, glasses. One fool of a man had taken her back to a campsite she had already checked to point out an anaemic Norwegian.

Molly went on around the field. Only when there were no older women or children present did she investigate. A younger woman present, yes, for Molly had acquired out of a need to render her intended victim as detestable as possible the suspicion that Donald Morgan had some cheap tart in tow even as his wife sweated in the death cell.

Circuit of the field completed, Molly went back to her car, a plain black saloon of a common make and year, and bearing false plates. She took off her shoulder bag, sat for a moment before making a move.

Molly was tired. The journey from London having taken only half as long as expected, she had arrived near Exeter in the middle of the night and had needed to wait out hours of darkness, parked, dozing between eras filled with cigarettes and retreats from gloom.

Stretching the flesh around her eyes, Molly started the engine. She drove on along the country road for whose prettiness she had no mind. Within minutes she was slowing: large orange tent in a paddock. She speeded up again when a boy and a dog came bounding into view.

As Molly drove, scanning about, that suspicion in respect of Donald Morgan and another woman developed nicely. The tart, a convicted child abuser, had been involved from before the start, the publicly known. It was for her that Morgan had got his wife to help him disappear by killing someone, a disappearance necessitated by a big swindle he had worked on his best friend, and had then tricked her into taking the blame. He was truly evil, that bastard.

Following signposts to another official camping ground, Molly parked on a dirt lane. She got out with her shoulder bag, locked the car, entered a field, began to walk along beside the line of tents.

Although Molly did think Donald Morgan could be alive, not even momentarily did she believe she was going to find him. It didn't matter. She could keep it up for days, the search; for days or weeks or months; not driving around all the time but working, dwelling on the task. She would make it live.

Bran was whistling as he drove. This had never been one of his habits but it now prevented a flowering of his embarrassment over the fact of his being here, in the Exeter area. The tune had been a popular hit for weeks and he despised it.

Bran idled the car along, whereas on the journey he had driven at dangerous speed. The latter's motivation he had ignored, the former's he was impatiently aware of: what could he say to Mrs. James Morgan when he got to the orchard?

Bran kept on considering it. He still didn't know, was

still not taking the right final direction, when he saw
Molly Harker go driving by.

He had stopped in the roadside at a country junction to
get a bee out of the car. That done, he was preparing to
move on, go straight across, when a car came from the
right. At its wheel was the woman who, he snap-recalled,
had been the person to ask him, "Don't you think there's
something funny about that Orchard thing?"

Shocked, his mouth in no shape for whistling, Bran
drove to the left, followed the black car. He could feel his
heartbeat. What was happening he had no notion or
guess, he was putting no twos together, but he did know
that whatever impulse of instinct or shrewdness or pre-
science brought him here had been totally right.

Over the following hour Bran calmed to happily tense.
He stayed well back from the car ahead, sometimes allowing other vehicles to come between. From the way
Molly Harker hesitated at junctions and from her dawdle
he got the impression she had no particular aim, was perhaps looking for some kind of landmark.

At noon, in a one-street village, the black car stopped.
Molly went into a snack bar. Going on foot as close as he
dared, feeling sure that being spotted could spoil everything, Bran saw the woman mundanely eating a sandwich.
He belched with a hunger he had just discovered.

Retreating, he found a baker's and bought its sole remaining item, a small brown loaf, which he ate back in
the car while not thinking of a complementing pint of
cool foamy beer.

Molly came out, drove on. Her next halt was at a camping site. Again she locked her car and carried a shoulder
bag. She went into the camp to wander among the tents
and motor caravans. There was nothing to be read from

her expression. She came out to the car and drove off. Though he didn't understand her actions, Bran had no feeling that he was wasting his time.

The thin scream shot through the air, anguish given voice. It was over before Donald recognised car brakes squealing. He had thought he was hearing the cry of a wounded animal, maybe a rabbit caught in a snare. Recognition brought relief: he couldn't stand the thought of small creatures being hurt.

Crawling to the tent front on all-fours Donald looked out and down, down toward the road a hundred yards away. There, a car had stopped, dust beginning to rise. From the same direction another car appeared. It went on by as the first one's door was opening. A woman, sole passenger, got out and walked back toward the gate.

Call of nature, Donald thought, withdrawing inside the tent, whereupon he wondered if this could be the field's owner. He swung forward again to put his head through the flap.

Pushing the gate open the woman came through. Donald, prepared to withdraw like a flash if she embarked on private doings, watched her as she came on, walking up the incline. There was nothing about her out of the ordinary, he reflected, unless it was a whiff of familiarity, which you got a lot of nowadays, women all seemed to wear the same clothes and have the same hair styles.

Since it appeared that the woman was coming here, or at any rate would pass close if going for a walk, Donald, who was stripped to his khaki shorts, sat on his heels and reached for a shirt. When he had it on he crawled outside. He got up.

It was like a finger jabbing under the breastbone, the

sensation Donald got on recognising the woman, who had come to a halt some ten feet away. He stared at her face with its tired sort of smile; stared while trying to make sense of her being here but reminding himself that there was nothing for him to worry about.

She said a flat, "Donald Morgan."

He asked, "What d'you want?"

"Remember me?"

"No."

"That could be true," she said. "Hold on." She bent to her shoulder bag.

Beside the field that rose gently to the crest on which stood a tent, there were trees, the dwindle edge of a wood. Through these trees crept Bran.

By now his heart should have settled from its spurt of alarm when he had rounded the bend to find Molly Harker parked there, though she wasn't trying a trap, she granted him not a glance as he went past with one hand over his face; but the thudding in his chest was going on.

Bran didn't know why it should be. The man who had come out of the tent was probably the common-law husband, Henry Gosport. But if he was, this bucolic angle sat strangely with an East End gangster, to mention nothing of his girl friend, so a robbery or other criminal act could be in the air, which would mean that a snooper could be in danger of losing his life.

Bran stopped moving, a hand on a tree for steadiness. He nodded at the information he gave himself, that the wisest thing he could do was quietly retreat and stake the situation out from a secure vantage point.

In peering through intervening trees, a last look before backing off, Bran saw that Molly Harker was holding a gun. To try to find out what this meant he switched to the man, who had half turned away, this way, as though wary. The man was Donald Morgan. In spite of having semi-believed in the existence of the man since hearing of his wife's claim, Bran was staggered.

Mouth open, he told himself, It's Donald Morgan. That one there. He's Donald Morgan. He's supposed to be dead and he's not. He's alive. He's Donald Morgan. His wife's going to hang at eight o'clock in the morning for having murdered him. Donald Morgan.

Trembling, his heart throwing madman punches, Bran turned and started to move away at a crouch. He thought, Please God let me be first with the news I'll never ask for anything else as long as I live.

"I imagine that's another toy," Donald Morgan had said, sounding cool even though his stance was changing and his suntan had gone yellow.

Why Molly hadn't answered immediately was because of her suspicion that she had heard something significant. Giving up trying to think what, she said, "It's real and it's loaded. Be careful what you do."

"I'm always careful."

"You remember me now, eh?"

Voice less cool: "Maybe."

"Sure you do. I came to your house."

"Well?"

Molly said, "I asked for a tiny bit of help. Asked you to tell the truth. Not much to ask, that."

"What d'you want here?"

"Molly Harker's the name."

"I was just leaving."

He looked as though he thought he was already doing

that, Molly mused, standing there sideways. It was something. Be better if he got down on his knees.

Molly felt oddly disappointed, low. She knew it had little to do with the man's attitude, but that would serve, if her feeling wasn't due to the fact that she was about to kill someone.

She asked, "Where's the girl friend?"

He frowned. "My what?"

"Never mind. Doesn't matter. Just so long as you know why you're getting it."

"Getting it?"

"You know what I mean."

That he did, that furthermore it was deserved, the revenge, showed in his eyes and in the high rise of fear in his voice when he spoke. He said, "This is handy. You can give me a lift to town."

It was a good try, Molly allowed while weighing form, noting all the inflammable items around as well as a plentiful supply of wood, seeing that the fire ought to be made farther back where it wouldn't be seen from the road.

Better taken than dragged, she thought before saying, "Move on, Morgan. Over there."

"What for?"

"If you don't move I'll kill you."

"This is silly," he said in a little-boy tone, moving.

Molly followed. With the road gone from view she ordered Morgan to stop. When he had obeyed and turned, shoulders hunched, hands holding each other by his waist, colour a touch of jaundice, she said, "Good-bye."

Lurching his torso forward Donald Morgan blurted, "It was self-defence."

Molly fired. Morgan, four feet away, was jolted backwards. He crashed to the ground. After his limbs had settled he lay still. He was clearly dead.

Reckoning she was reacting to the pain in her wrist and biceps from the gun's kick, Molly began to sob. She went on doing so as she set about pulling across the tent and camping gear. By the time these were piled on top of the body and she was fetching wood, she was crying fit to break a heart.

The truck that killed Bran Peel, it came upon him so quickly at the junction where he should have slowed, he never had time even to feel alarm.

About the Author

Mark McShane's previous novels for the Crime Club, written under his pseudonym "Marc Lovell," include *Comfort Me With Spies, Good Spies Don't Grow on Trees,* and *Apple Spy in the Sky,* which was released as the film *The Trouble with Spies.* Under his own name, he is the author of many other novels, the best known of which was made into an award-winning film, *Seance on a Wet Afternoon.* He has lived on Majorca for nearly thirty years.